TABLEAUX

TABLEAUX
Scenes from the Decade of Excess

Dominic Jay

CIRCA

If you were queen of pleasure,
And I were king of pain,
We'd hunt down love together,
Pluck out his flying-feather,
And teach his feet a measure,
And find his mouth a rein;
If you were queen of pleasure,
And I were king of pain.

Algernon Charles Swinburne,
A Match

The events in this story take place
between August 1984 and January 1985.
Some characters are real, others imagined.
It is left to the reader to decide which
is which.

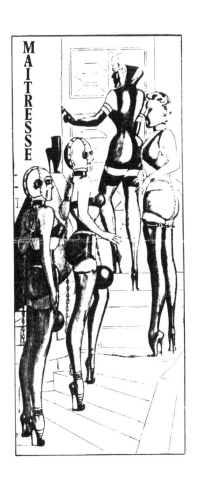

August 1984

1

Rain strafed the ground so violently that it rebounded to her knees. Darting between the stationary traffic, she sought shelter in the nearest doorway. Her sodden dress clung to her, brazenly diaphanous. Heavens, the sky really had fallen on her head. But the air smelt so sweet. Another hour of that leaden humidity and she might have expired. She sloughed off her heels and let her toes play on the cool marble step. God, it felt good.

Her bag was a write-off, but what about her cigarettes? No ... somehow they'd survived. She lit up, adding a lungful of toxins to the roll of afternoon delights.

Smoking contentedly, she picked out a distant figure in a morning suit wading up the street. His tails snapped at his legs, and he held his soggy hat with evident disdain. As he approached, he patted his pockets with his free hand, miming a quest for a key. He paused and stared. 'Sorry, am I in your way?' she said.

'I suppose you are, rather ... this is my front door.'

With his hair slicked back there was a hint of Bowie's Thin White Duke. Blue eyes, high forehead, aquiline nose. Not at all bad. She moved aside to let him in. He'd almost closed the door when he appeared to have a change of heart.

'How rude of me', he said, suddenly all smiles. 'I quite forgot my manners. Perhaps you'd like to come up and dry out? I can offer you a coffee ...'

Was that a euphemism? No, he didn't look the type. But it might be fun to pat him about a bit and see which way he jumped. She flicked her cigarette into the gutter and followed him inside.

'Come in', he said. 'You'll have to excuse the mess. I'm Oliver, by the way ... Oliver Woolf.'

'Candy', she replied.

'Like Candy Darling?'

'Uh-huh ...'

'The bathroom's through there if you want to take off your things.'

'I'm fine, thanks. I'd just like to dry my hair.'

He returned with a towel, then left the room again without comment. She heard a kettle being filled and set on the stove and then nothing.

What to make of him? He was tall and pretty enough, early thirties, maybe less. He sounded like a toff, but the vibe was more New Romantic than Young Fogey. Mostly he looked like a kid with his nose against a sweetshop window, as if he hadn't had seen a woman in years. But the radar was picking up something. He couldn't be as colourless as he appeared.

2

He placed her. She was one of the window people. One of the regulars into whose lives he'd gained momentary insights from his vantage point on the second floor.

His street ran down towards Hyde Park, a positive, but lay too close to the human and motor traffic of Paddington station to be regarded as 'fashionable'. It was a scruffy, workaday London thoroughfare, though the location suited him, and he enjoyed its meagre attractions. The flat was his retreat. He never entertained there, partly because it was so small, but more importantly, because when he wanted company, he liked to venture out into the world.

He'd set his typewriter on an old campaign table by the window. The machine itself was brand new, a self-correcting IBM Selectric. It was so superior to his old Olivetti — a present from his grandfather when he'd gone up to Cambridge — that the guilt he bore for abandoning his old friend had been overwhelmed by the satisfaction he got from touching the IBM's keys and hearing the typeball whir. Before he began work in the morning he liked to sit at his desk with a coffee and a cigarette and watch the world go by.

He knew certain routines by heart: the hotel doorman arriving at six; the pharmacist opening at seven; the postman on his round; and the gaggle of working girls returning home. The afternoon presented a different cast of characters, of whom Candy was one. He had no idea where she went each day, only that her routine was constant and therefore unremarkable. She had become part of the scenery.

Close up, though, she was far more compelling. Her platinum hair hung limply, and her mascara ran in veins down her cheeks. Violated by the rain, she was gamine, but her face radiated strength and intelligence.

He changed into jeans and a T-shirt and left his damp morning things in a heap on the bedroom floor. When he rejoined Candy, she was perched tentatively on the edge of the sofa, as if trying not to leave a mark.

'I should have worn a rubber frock', she said; 'Rubber's perfect in the wet.' He smiled, not sure whether he should take her seriously. 'I hope your suit isn't ruined', she continued. A trace of an accent: estuarine or affectation?

'Oh, don't worry about that. It's Moss Bros. I've been to a wedding.'

'I prefer funerals ...'

'Me too. But I usually feel the same at both. Relieved that it's not mine. At least with a wedding you can go round again if you wish.'

'Was it a friend?'

'No, family ... my sister. And I'll put money on it not being her last. Actually, I found it all rather depressing.'

So, you've caught me with my defences down. And I've had far too much to drink, otherwise I would never have invited you in, he could have said, but did not.

Sister Holly had hitched herself to Henry Pound — 'Pink Pound' — PPS to one of Mrs T's leading wets and a rising Tory star. Famously ambitious, Henry was equally notorious for swinging both ways. Often simultaneously, in threes, fours, and fives. But word had come down from the PM that if he wanted to get ahead, then he'd better hurry up and get a wife and so Holly the popsicle had become an unwitting political beard.

'Just because you haven't found anyone nice, you want to spoil my fun too', was all she said when he'd tried to talk her out of it. Little idiot.

Candy cradled her coffee cup, and he noticed the elaborate silver knuckle ring on her left hand. Its overlapping plates suggested a fragment of a medieval jousting glove: her armour perhaps? Her eyes roamed the room as she drank. 'I like that', she said, pointing to a study of a coal miner in gouache and ink.

'It's by Henry Moore ... one of his war series. He gave it to my grandmother, and she left it to me.'

'Lucky you ... and this?'

One of his few precious objects was a porcelain bowl with a peacock glaze, which had emerged from the kiln slightly wonky. 'I call it my "rescue pot". It's a second, and it shouldn't have survived, but Lucie Rie gave it to me on condition I never try to sell it.'

'Wonky's always more interesting', she said. 'You've got some nice things ... but how come you have all these books?'

'I like to read. I find it's cheaper than therapy.'

'No, seriously, I've never known anyone with so many.'

'Well, I inherited a lot. I found a few in junk shops. Some are review copies. Others I stole, but I've managed to shake that habit. Almost anyway.'

'So, what do you do?'

'I'm a writer, or a journalist at any rate. I work on the *Telegraph*. I cover architecture and design mostly, but also art and anything else when they think it's too weird to warrant a piece by somebody serious ...'

He liked to tell people that he was a literary taxi driver, that he wrote for whoever flagged him down. Naturally, his family disapproved. They seemed to disapprove of everything he did. His grandfather accused him of wasting an expensive education; his father simply quoted his friend, Nicholas Tomalin: 'The only qualities essential for real success in journalism are rat-like cunning, a plausible manner and a little literary ability.' Oliver took pride in a score of at least two out of three.

He was a freelancer now: 'editor-at-large' they called it. Not that it made much difference. The one advantage was that it allowed him to work at home in peace and fax his copy instead of hammering away at an ancient office Remington, being drip-fed other people's conversations. Other than that, he'd always come and gone virtually as he pleased.

Her gaze had drifted back to the bookshelves, so he changed the subject: 'Wasn't Candy Darling a transsexual?'

'Uh-huh ... a t-girl. She started out as Mr James Lawrence Slattery of Long Island, USA.' Candy stood up, suddenly animated.

'She was quite fetching though', he said. 'You'd never have known.'

'She was a star. Beautiful, like Kim Novak.'

'But with Pat Nixon's nose!'

'Heh! You're smart ... how come you know that?'

'I wrote about Warhol once, for the paper.' He offered her a cigarette and lit for them both.

'She was too good for him. He chewed her up and spat her out, like all the others.'

'I saw *Flesh* at the ICA a few years back', he said. 'I was surprised. It was rather good. I had no idea that the life of a New York hustler could be so compelling.'

'You know it was improvised? But it feels natural, and Candy is divine.' She struck a Candy Darling pose: head up, one hand under her chin. 'It's one of my best films. What about you, do you have a favourite?'

'*Chelsea Girls*, probably', he said. 'Although I've only ever seen fragments of it ... I think the split screen idea is very clever. I like the idea of telling two stories simultaneously. Don't you think it strange that nobody else has tried it?'

'I guess telling one story is more than enough for most people.'

'I suppose you're right.'

'Okay, what's your worst Warhol movie?' she asked.

'That's much more difficult. There are so many to choose from.'

'Give me your shortlist ...'

'Well, *Sleep* is up there. Tedium elevated to an art form.'

'And ...'

'Well, for similar reasons I might add *Empire*, but there's something more captivating about that. I like the way the light gradually changes behind the building.'

'I'm guessing you're saving the worst till last, right?'

'Yes ... *Blow Job*! Thirty-five minutes of someone else's oral satisfaction is too much for me.'

Candy let out a smoky cackle. 'That's my worst one too! He's *so* faking it. You can tell from a mile away ... and I know all the tricks.'

She retrieved a paperback from the floor. 'We had to read this at school', she said, and put it back on the shelf. *Decline and Fall* was one of the books Oliver had liberated from Blackwell's as a student and held on to, more from a sense of guilt than enjoyment.

'I'm reading it again now', he said, 'though I'm not sure why. It's meant to be a satire, but I find it rather bleak.'

'I like bleak', she replied, 'especially when it happens to the right people, and Margot Beste-Chetwynde is a complete cow.'

'It's pronounced *beast-chained*.'

'No, you're not serious?' That wonderful laugh again.

'Absolutely, it's the funniest thing about the book, but it's never explained.'

'One of my clients is a novelist', she said. 'Mills and Boon. Says it's easy money. Maybe I should try it.'

'A client? So, what do you do?'

'I'm a tart', she said, matter of fact, much as you would say, 'I'm an accountant'.

'No, I had you down as a librarian', he said, only half joking.

A narrowing of the eyes. A twitch at the corners of the mouth. 'You don't approve?'

'No, no, I mean you don't match my mental image of someone who does what you say you do.'

'We come in all shapes and sizes you know. You'd be surprised.'

The rain stopped as abruptly as it had started, and Candy took it as her cue to leave. 'Come again', he called out, as she disappeared down the stairs, 'I really enjoyed our conversation.'

He went to pick up his book, then remembered that she'd put it back on the shelf. To his surprise, when he looked in the familiar place, there it was, in modern fiction under 'W'. How about that? Perhaps she was a librarian after all.

* * *

The following evening, he found a handwritten note lying on the doormat: *I have something for you. I'll try again tomorrow.* No name or signature.

She called again as promised. The buzzer sounded as he was hanging up his coat. 'I followed you up the street', she said, as she reached the top of the stairs. With her make-up intact she was devastating, a Punk Tippi Hedren. Her eyes signalled mischief and her mouth resisted a smile. Hitchcock would have adored her.

'Really … was that a coincidence or were you expecting me?'

'Just chance. I was coming to see you anyway.'

'Can I offer you a drink, or is it too early?'

'Never too early. Maybe a vodka if you've got some. I've brought you this.' With a flourish, she revealed a thin square parcel, beautifully wrapped in silver paper. She presented it on her fingertips, as if it were a salver. 'I hope you'll like it … go on, open it!'

He peeled off the tape, careful not to tear the paper. Inside was a copy of *The Velvet Underground*, still in its cellophane wrapper. 'Thank you! And how clever of you. How did you know I hadn't got it?'

'I looked through your records while you were changing the other day', she said. 'It was easy. You organise them alphabetically, like your books. I popped into Vinyl Solutions on Portobello … maybe you know it? It's run by a creepy old Nazi, but he has all the best stuff.'

'You really are wonderful', he said. 'Let's listen to it now. How long have you got?'

'Oh, maybe an hour. Long enough. I don't have to be out again until eight, but it can take a while to get ready.'

He sliced through the cellophane with his thumbnail and slipped the disc from its sleeve. Placing it on the turntable, he lowered the stylus over the start of the first track:

Candy says I've come to hate my body
and all that it requires in this world …

When she'd gone, he settled at the typewriter. The street was so narrow that from where he sat, he looked directly into the hotel rooms opposite. In the evening, the windows would light up at random, like an X-rated Advent calendar. Often, he found himself a willing voyeur, an accessory after the fact of other people's sex lives.

The couple in the room opposite had been providing entertainment for the past twenty minutes. A skinny blonde sat astride a man whose bald pate glistened under the harsh fluorescent light. How much longer were they going to keep it up? Then she saw him and waved. Another pro.

* * *

'So, I waved back, then pulled down the blind …' He related the story over dinner, sitting on Jan's terrace with a bottle of Frascati and a take-away Chinese. Jan was his oldest friend. A Czech architect with a sharp eye, and an acute sense of the absurd, he drew like an angel and pictured the future in a more compelling way than anyone Oliver knew. Sensuous, priapic forms emerged from his mind and leapt effortlessly onto paper.

The second he'd finished telling Jan about the evening's peep show, his friend asked: 'So what's the gossip?' Jan thrived on intrigue. It was one of the qualities that made him enemies but endeared him to his friends.

'Well, you'll never guess what happened to me?'

'They fired you at last?'

'Ha ha … not as far as I know. No, I came home the other day to find a tart on my doorstep. Soaking wet.'

'Really?' said Jan, lowering his glass. 'You're not serious?'

'Perfectly serious. And you know what? I invited her in!'

'No. I don't believe it!'

'And this afternoon she came to see me again …'

He told Jan everything, elaborating for effect here and there. Walking home afterwards, though, he regretted his braggadocio. He'd made Candy sound like some sort of flotsam. But she was bright and engaging; and had he been honest, he'd have admitted to a budding affection for her. But then the truth wouldn't have made anything like as good a story.

3

Whatever made her say she was a tart? True, she'd given enough head in her time, though one swallow doesn't make a summer, as they say. She'd wanted to shock, obviously. But Oliver had been more puzzled than anything, poor boy. If he only knew half of what she really got up to he'd be rocked to his socks. But then again, maybe not. Scratch most English public-school boys and you'll find a willing submissive. And Oliver surely had potential in that department.

The LP she'd chosen was a favourite. Better than that, it included the track she connected with more than any other — *Candy Says*. She sang it as she walked, certain that Lou Reed had written it as a love song.

In their orbit around Warhol, each of the Superstars had basked in their moment of fame. But the closer they flew, the more likely they were to singe their wings; and Candy Darling had been vulnerable from the start. She felt alienated and projected that feeling on to others. Candy understood instinctively; but alienation could also be a source of inspiration. That was how she was able to empathise so effectively with her clients.

Her route to work took her along the canal towpath towards the broad expanse of Paddington Basin. A motley collection of narrow boats stood about idly, their decks a colourscape of geraniums and zinnias. She marvelled at how otherwise perfectly sane people managed to live on the boats. How cramped it must be; how cold in winter; how ghastly not to have a proper lav. 'Jesus, sometimes I sound like my mother.'

Her rooms were on the first floor of a Victorian villa, an oddity, located at the end of a long stucco-fronted terrace. The neighbouring properties had been carved into bedsits or brothels, often both. London's oldest cathouse was a few doors down, at number 69. Truly, you couldn't make it up. And all courtesy of their lordships, the Church Commissioners, freeholders of the entire district.

When Candy first saw the villa, its grand rooms had been full of the junk some ancient dowager had left behind. Olga, the landlady, had conned the old bat out of the lease, canny cow.

Olga Taussig was old-school, with blue-chip connections. She'd been *the* Society madam in the Sixties. Her trick had been to recruit middle-class girls who weren't too attached to their knickers: 'Only ever deal posh pussy darling. You get a much better return on your investment.'

Olga's tarts were delivered by limo, dolled up to the nines and decked out in pearls. And the cash had rolled in. She was retired now, living between London and Tel Aviv, but even so there wasn't an embassy or a hotel in the West End where she hadn't got some kind of 'in'.

The villa was a base for what Olga called the Privilege Club. It wasn't really a club at all, simply a network of kinksters who communicated through small ads in the *Times* and *Exchange & Mart*. Olga had a flat in the attic, and used the ground floor for parties, but sublet the rest of the house to girls she liked.

Candy's rooms were a realm where the imagination had free rein. Her clients ranged from the masochistic, through the submissive, to the downright peculiar, the distinctions sometimes being hard to define. Most wanted to explore a fetish, or role-play with a sympathetic partner. A few paid extravagant sums just to be abused, and then the privilege was shared.

The realisation that there was a living to be made from something she enjoyed had come one evening during a break at *La Vie en Rose*. She'd been dressed for a can-can routine, in patent-leather thigh-highs with mad heels. She'd thrown a mackintosh over her costume and slipped out to the caff behind the Windmill for soup and a cigarette.

Sitting there, she noticed a guy gawping at her feet. Eventually he leaned across and said: 'Pardon me, Mistress, will you allow me to polish your boots?' He looked downtrodden: browbeaten at home and bullied at work. But why not? While she smoked, he fumbled under the table. It was distracting, but not disagreeable. Eventually he zipped himself up and placed a banknote on the table. Twenty quid was as much as she earned a night as a dancer and she'd made it in fifteen minutes, without even having to stand up. A business opportunity beckoned.

Candy Darling said that the name you choose for yourself is more your own than the one you're born with: how true. Candy could claim three, only one of which no longer belonged. She had been born Catherine, but Catherine had begat Candy, had begat Candide. She was Catherine to family, her neighbours, and the bank; Candy to her friends; and Candide professionally. Those who knew Catherine would never imagine Mistress Candide; and those who knew Candy by day might conceivably not recognise her at night.

Candy had sprung into the world as a teenager, almost fully formed. Her emergence as a Punk was a simple act of rebellion, a sharp rebuttal of Catherine and the suffocating social code that bound her family and her class. Candide, in contrast, had developed from a far more considered exploration.

The spark had been seeing Bulle Ogier in *Maîtresse*. Ariane the dominatrix had excited her viscerally, offering a vision of a world she hadn't known existed. And once set free there was no turning back. She must have seen the film a dozen times and always noted something new. The only detail she'd never been able to put in place was the Gérard Depardieu character: the brute lover. She was still waiting for that special someone to break into her life.

Ariane had been her starting point. Then, like little Jimmy Slattery, holed up in Massapequa Park waiting to shed his chrysalis and flutter away as Candy Darling, she'd spent time studying the field. But whereas Jimmy had fixated on blondes, she'd been drawn to the darker end of the spectrum, bracketing herself between two raven-haired icons: Bettie Page and Louise Brooks — Lulu. From Bettie she took all the superficial goodies of the trade:

the stockings and heels, the gloves, and the corsets. But Lulu's influence was more profound. She offered a role model: a woman for whom life holds no fears.

'I have a gift for enraging people', Lulu said. 'But if I ever bore you, it'll be with a knife.' You don't argue with a girl like that.

* * *

Wherever she was professionally in the evening, Candy aimed to leave before twelve, her personal witching hour. Then depending on the night of the week, or whether she was feeling up or down (enhanced or not), she would go on to one of her regular clubs — Der Putsch, Maitresse, or Submission. That was how she'd acquired her maid, Margrét, who attached herself one night at Der Putsch and stuck like glue.

Margrét was a novice then and desperate for attention. It hadn't taken long to see how a stray little kitty like her might be put to good use. Now she looked after the rooms and attended to clients. Apart from weekends, she was always on duty. In return, she was guided in the dark arts of domination.

The contract between maid and mistress is simple: the employee has no rights and the employer no obligations. However, the small print introduces line after line of emotional insecurities, which can result in frequent incidences of mutiny and balancing oppression.

Candy had devised numerous ways of maintaining control. Margrét's costume, inspired by a French hotel maid's uniform, was particularly effective, having been designed to optimise discomfort. Black rubber stockings complemented a short black rubber dress, with a frilled underskirt, a cap, apron, and bloomers, all in white. On top of this ensemble, she wore a boned corset that made it impossible to bend at the waist. The final detail was a pair of boots with hazardous heels, which introduced a constant element of instability. Candy enjoyed the rustling of latex and creaking of leather as Margrét went about her tasks. When night duty demanded it, she could be confined in this uniform for up to sixteen hours.

The French windows swung open to release the bright sounds of birdsong. It was unusual for Candy to be in her rooms before two o'clock, but that morning she had to attend to a Justice of the High Court, whose punishment had involved his detention overnight.

It fell to Margrét to unbuckle the straps that secured the judge to the Catherine Wheel, a rotating device of Candy's own design. She had gone home, leaving Margrét with instructions to turn the wheel, and strike the old man regularly on the quarter hour. It was an elegant arrangement in that it succeeded in depriving them both of sleep.

'You may go now', she said.

'Thank you, Mistress', the judge said quietly when his hood was removed. When in role, she allowed no one to address her, other than to acknowledge a command or offer gratitude, as the pathetic figure before her had just done.

'When you're ready, Margrét will run you a bath.'

Margrét turned and glared, then cast her eyes down at the floor obediently.

'Yes, Mistress', she said.

Candy looked through the appointments for the coming week. Among her regulars, she counted several literary figures, a racing driver, a minor royal, and a veteran Labour MP, the latter a person of particularly savage tastes. Each of them had a *nom de scène*, which was allocated on the first visit and used thereafter.

To ensure discretion, she made it a rule never to receive more than one client in an afternoon. Today's treat was the Toad, a tabloid proprietor and a flyblown brute of a man. Coincidentally, it had been on the way home from a particularly inventive session with the Toad that she'd first bumped into Oliver, which made the afternoon memorable in all kinds of ways.

She took the role seriously, which was why she was so successful. If a client had a specific fantasy that he or she wished to explore, she would dress and accessorise accordingly. The episode with the boot fetishist in the caff had shown that the more theatrical the make-up and more exotic the costume, the more positive the response, and so dressing up had become a way of life.

For the Toad, she'd selected a 'bootsuit' — stiletto-heeled boots and catsuit all in one — made by her friends at AtomAge. The longer she wore it, the hotter she got; and the hotter she grew the more sadistic she became: a perfect outcome. The leather was supple and fitted like a second skin. She ran a hand over the slippery surface and her muscles flexed beneath it.

To darken the mood further, she wore a black wig, cut in a Lulu bob. Satisfied, she stood in front of the mirror and combed her new helmet of hair to glossy perfection. Finally, she applied ruby red lipstick, and eyeliner in a trademark shade of midnight. The transformation to Mistress Candide was complete ... *et tout est pour le mieux dans le meilleur des mondes possibles.* She smiled at the face in the mirror and blew herself a kiss.

September 1984

4

The familiar black Bentley was waiting outside the club, its engine running silently. Candy slid onto the back seat and the door closed with a refined *thunk*. The Storekeeper — her coinage, not his — pressed a button beneath the dividing screen and spoke to the uniformed thug behind the wheel: 'Grosvenor Square, and then you can park up. I won't need you again tonight.' It was his third appointment in a month and the first time she'd agreed to go home with him. And only then because the money was so flippin' good.

She'd made a New Year's resolution to give up the late-night sessions, but it wasn't that simple. She enjoyed the random encounters, the dances with danger; she thrived on the adrenaline rush. Maybe give it a few more years. Thirty was a nice round number to go out on. She'd have had enough of it by then anyway.

The limousine surged forward, and the gloom of Shaftesbury Avenue gave way to the neon Neverland of Piccadilly Circus. She gazed out at the artificial ad-scape, not bothering to hide her boredom. She liked the car though. An open humidor revealed a cache of Cohiba Siglos, and beneath the scent of fresh cigars were notes of warm leather and conditioned air. A gentleman's club on the move. Except that the Storekeeper was no gentleman. You can't buy class, darlin'.

The driver had his window down and his breath formed a mist in the cold night air. He lit a fag, and the mist became a cloud. Absentmindedly, she fixated on the dark mat of hair on the back of his neck. Maybe it covered his shoulders too, perhaps his whole body? Heavens, what a creature: a Neanderthal. She looked up and caught him eyeing her hungrily in the mirror. She winked, as if to say, 'in your dreams'.

'Let me take your things …' The Storekeeper was being incredibly attentive, Mister Geniality. His sitting room was as vulgar as its size implied, furnished like the Ritz, and stocked like an onanist's emporium, with Oriental and Indian erotica.

An exquisite Mughal *Kama Sutra* lay open on the coffee table, its gilded plates beckoning. Next to it sat a leather-bound copy of the Marquis de Sade's *Justine*. A pair of white cotton gloves encouraged exploration, but she resisted. All she wanted was to acquit herself professionally and leave: 'Excuse me, I just need to pop to the lav.'

She turned the latch on the bathroom door and set the toilet seat down noisily, removed a sachet from her powder compact and cut a neat line on top of the cistern. She took it in one go, dabbed away any traces from her nose, washed her hands, wiped the cistern with the damp towel, and flushed. All in the time it would have taken to pee.

When she returned, he was standing by the drinks cabinet, proprietorially, glass in hand. 'What can I get you?'

'Nothing, thanks. I'm fine.' She took out a cigarette and he responded immediately with the offer of a lighter: an elaborate gold affair that sent up a tall blue flame.

'I see you're interested in my collection', he said. 'Perhaps you've read the Marquis?' He handed her *Justine*. 'This is very special ... from the first edition of 1791.'

She balanced her cigarette on the edge of the ashtray and examined the little book, turning its pages delicately. It was an exquisite thing with engraved illustrations, each depicting some form of supposed sexual depravity. She paused to pick up her cigarette again.

'How interesting that you should stop there', he said, looking over her shoulder. It was a dungeon scene, depicting a woman in the act of pulling away a stool from beneath a naked suspendee. The grateful wretch was ejaculating in response to the tightening noose.

'Asphyxiophilia ... erotic asphyxiation', he continued. 'Compressing the carotid arteries, as in strangulation or hanging, results in acute loss of oxygen to the brain. Ultimately, it leads to death but in the interim, it induces a euphoric state, not unlike a cocaine rush.' So, he knew exactly what she'd been up to in the bathroom.

She drew on her cigarette and pictured the scene — his naked form dangling from the ceiling, penis erect — and for a moment imagined him clawing at the rope, eyes popping and tongue protruding, before the final gargle of death. The perfect crime. Except that his driver knew they'd gone up to the flat together, so they'd catch up with her eventually. A pity. He deserved it.

'Combined with orgasm, I find it most exhilarating ... and equally addictive from both perspectives. I sense that you're a woman with a profoundly dominant instinct. I believe you might enjoy a little experimentation. Am I right?'

So that was the evening's entertainment: his life in her hands.

5

The low morning sun cast a golden light on the smog that shrouded Trafalgar Square. The effect seemed to encapsulate certain aspects of the city's character: gloomy yet mysterious; hazardous yet romantic. Monet said that London would have been ugly were it not for the fog. Oliver squinted and tried to imagine how the master would have recorded the scene before him.

His eye fixed on a point of colour approaching along Whitehall. It was a girl on a Lambretta, her boots, jacket, and helmet all perfectly coordinated with the lipstick-pink of the scooter. She wove confidently through the traffic, a vivid counterpoint to the red and black of the buses and taxis. Then she was gone.

He made his way through the traffic to the centre of the square and the stinking squatter camp of pigeons. As a boy he'd perfected the technique of catching his toe beneath the tail of an unsuspecting bird and lifting it high into the air. He was tempted to try it again, but knew he'd be too slow, even if he could bear the embarrassment of being caught.

From the square it was a short walk to the London Library. He'd never joined a club. Instead, he had the library, which charged him £60 a year. For that, he had a retreat from the hubbub of the city, a place to read and to work in peace. Drinking and talking he preferred to do in bars.

Occasionally in the library he encountered writers he knew. Like a twitcher, he enjoyed studying these rare birds in their natural habitat, noting their foibles. John Betjeman used to fuss about amiably, before shuffling off for good; Kingsley Amis made far too much noise, as if he owned the place. Bruce Chatwin, true to form, habitually sought an audience. One person would do.

Sitting in a quiet corner of the bookstacks, Bruce opened his Moleskine notebook, revealing page after page of beautifully handwritten manuscript, and asked if he'd like to hear the latest instalment. Indeed, he would. And in any case one could never say no to Bruce. He was so charismatic, and so apparently guileless, that nobody could look into those ice-blue eyes and refuse him anything.

'The Ancients sang their way all over the world. They sang the rivers and ranges, saltpans and sand dunes. They hunted, ate, made love, danced, killed: wherever their tracks led they left a trail of music ...' When he'd finished reading, he waited for a reaction.

'I think it's wonderful: tell me about it.'

'Man is a talking creature, a singing creature. The first language must have been in song, relying on sounds before there were words. Australian Aboriginals believe that as each of the ancestors took his first step forward, he sang his name. The name was the beginning of a song, which unfolded with the second step and then the third and so on. Slowly, as they traced a pathway through the land, they sang their world into being.'

'I think I understand', Oliver said, though in truth he didn't: 'What are you going to call it?'

'Well, I began with *Of the Nomads: A Discourse*, but I think that's possibly a little dry, don't you?'

'It sounds like the title of a Royal Geographical Society lecture.'

'I know ... that's what I like about it.'

'Do you have an alternative?'

'Well, the Aboriginal people call these pathways the *Footprints of the Ancestors* or the *Way of the Law*. But Europeans call them *Songlines*. I may use that.'

Bruce could pluck tales from the air. Like a medieval storyteller, he elaborated in the telling and retelling, to the point where if indeed a line existed between fact and fiction, it was no longer of interest. The narrative was everything. It was a truth in and of itself. In South Africa he'd had the extraordinary luck to be present at the excavation of what was believed to be the earliest known hearth, in a cave at Swartkrans, a remote place, rich with hominid remains. Recounting the story, he made the moment of discovery — of stepping back in time two million years — more thrilling, the tell-tale charred fragment of antelope bone more fragile, its significance more profound.

'Can you picture it? Possibly the most important paleontological find in a century and all he says is' — he adopted a laconic South African accent — *That bone is remarkably suggestive*. He smiled. Bruce was a fabulous mimic. Noël Coward was his party piece and he had Jackie O to a T. Jackie was a friend, by the way, in case you didn't know. Bruce's technique involved much more than perfecting the voice. Somehow, he managed to project an entire persona. 'Imagine if Archimedes had been South African. No Eureka moment for him! No running through the streets of Syracuse naked!'

'They're a dry lot', Oliver said, 'like their biltong', but Bruce pretended not to hear.

'To be there at the moment of revelation: the very spot on which Prometheus seized the fire from Zeus and gifted it to Man. The terrain on which civilisation was born, where the hunted became the hunters. It was humbling ...'

The notion of Bruce being humbled by anything was stretching the imagination a little too far.

Bruce tied up his duffle bag and slung his jacket over his shoulder. 'I must be going', he said. 'But you should come and see my new place. You might like to write about it. Come tonight if you can.'

'I'd like that very much', said Oliver, and scribbled down the address. 'Does seven-thirty suit you?'

'Perfect ... I'll prepare something light. I'm leaving for Crete tomorrow. You know I can't bear to stay in this country for more than a week. One feels as if it's in the grip of some very dark forces.'

'You mean the miners?'

'No! I mean Mrs Godawful Thatcher and her creeping police state. She's just like Galtieri. If the Malvinas had gone against her, she'd be where he is now, and she knows it. She's an instinctive gambler. The miners are merely another throw of the dice. But the stakes are far higher this time. If she loses, the whole rotten political system is going to implode and take her with it.'

Lions led by donkeys, Oliver thought, but let it pass.

Turning the corner, back into Trafalgar Square, he found the traffic at a standstill. A bus stood skewed across the road, its front wheels mounted on the pavement. He should have turned away, but he maintained a childish superstition of detours as if, like walking beneath a ladder, or treading on the cracks in the pavement, to change course, once set, would bring bad luck.

The bus was full, but nobody appeared able or willing to get off. Then it struck him: the pink Lambretta. A policeman held aloft a crushed motorcycle helmet, as if he were a priest charged with a reliquary. Oliver froze, and the scene fell into silence, the only surviving sound being the vigorous, angry voice of Nina Simone on his Walkman:

… I sing, I sing, I sing, I sing
I sing, just to know that I'm alive

* * *

Bruce's apartment had been designed by a Minimalist, who described it as 'an architecture of almost nothing'. The space itself measured perhaps twenty feet by twenty feet. A tiny white cell. It might have been a monastic retreat, not that Bruce had ever been much of a monk.

As an acquirer of objects, Bruce was a bulimic, cyclically gorging and purging. The move to the flat had corresponded with a moment of purity in which virtually everything had been discarded. But he was already on the way up, rapidly introducing new finds, each with its own narrative. Alongside an Empire sofa and an Aalto table, which drew no comment, there was a campaign bed, on which Maréchal Ney — 'Napoleon's bravest of the brave' — was reputed to have slept, and an eighteenth-century chandelier, rescued from a manor house in southern Sweden, which was far too grand and hopelessly impractical, and left tiny gobbets of wax on the floor.

Smaller, more precious treasures were squirrelled away behind the scenes, each one a trophy of Bruce's connoisseur eye. He delighted in revealing and explaining each piece in turn. It was a live-in cabinet of curiosities, a raconteur's dressing-up box.

With Bruce, every action was a prompt for a fresh story. Cooking was no exception. He was preparing what he called *Brouillade de Truffes* — a dish of eggs and grated black truffle. 'I discovered this in Grasse', he said. 'We drove to a little place up in the hills. It was impossibly rustic, but the food was divine. They make it with duck eggs ... these are fresh from the farm. And I smuggled the truffle in my rucksack.' Oliver suspected Harrods Food Hall. 'They served it with quite a good Margaux, but we can have something a little more special.' Bruce pointed to a decanter. 'A Château Palmer '61 ... do you know it?'

'No, I'm ashamed to say I don't.'

'It's one of the great legends of Bordeaux, and very difficult to find now. Jonathan Cape sent me half a case at Christmas — this is bottle number five.'

Bruce handed him an elaborately cut glass, another *find* with a tale attached. 'I discovered these in a flea market in Montparnasse. They're from an Imperial Russian service made for Grand Duke Nicholas Nikolaevich in the middle of the last century ... you see it has his monogram HH.'

Oliver raised the liquid to the light and sniffed. He didn't have much of a nose, but even he could tell that he was in the presence of greatness.

'It feels incredibly vigorous for a wine more than twenty years old, don't you think?', asked Bruce. 'Their secret is to emphasise the Merlot in the mix. It has raspberry notes and there's a hint of violet ...'

He took another sip. What would it be like to have just one tenth of Bruce's élan?

Propped against the wall in one corner of the bedroom was the Mapplethorpe portrait, shot when Bruce was young and beautiful. 'I should get rid of that thing', he said. 'I feel it's reproaching me, like Dorian Gray.'

'We all grow old', said Oliver, knowing that wasn't the point.

'And the older one gets, the more one's face reveals … here, I'll show you.' Bruce pulled a leather-bound portfolio from beneath the divan. 'These are all by Mapplethorpe', he said. 'He gave them to me last time I was there.' Which was probably code for 'I stole them while he wasn't looking'. There were four portraits: an aged Louise Bourgeois, gleefully holding a huge bronze penis and balls; Truman Capote, every inch the dissolute dwarf; a sly-looking Andy Warhol; and a Punk girl in a ripped plastic dress.

He stared at the photograph of the girl. Slits in the dress revealed pierced nipples with lengths of silver chain strung between them, like a displaced necklace. Her hair was teased up in spikes and her make-up daubed on, but even in black and white the familiar eyes shone out.

'Bob discovered her in the Hellfire', said Bruce, holding the print delicately by the corners. 'Don't you think she's wonderful? She's almost certainly underage, but her face gives nothing away.'

'I know her', Oliver said. 'She turned up on my doorstep one afternoon and I took her in. She's a hooker.'

'It gets better and better', said Bruce. 'What a fascinating boy you are!'

* * *

Oliver settled into his seat on the Tube, thankful for the warmth of the carriage. Bruce had proposed that he write about the apartment for *Harpers & Queen* — he called it *Drama Queens* — but they would want a personality piece: 'Bruce Chatwin at home', 'the writer in his retreat', that sort of thing; and he wasn't really interested in pandering to Bruce's ego, which in any case appeared to have entered a particularly frangible phase.

The evening had ended on a maudlin note. Bruce had related how in Australia he'd picked up a copy of *Time* magazine only to find his portrait juxtaposed with an article on what they'd called the 'gay plague'. You could see why someone as superstitious as Bruce would find the connection morbid. Journalists could be such arseholes.

One thing he really hadn't wanted to pursue was a dissection of Bruce's sex life, past or present. Bruce was voracious: a compulsive. It didn't matter whether you were male or female, attached or single. And Bruce was so needy, he always wanted to suck you dry. But his genius was to turn friends into lovers and lovers into friends, so no one ever seemed to mind. The only complicating factor was the transition between the two camps, which fluctuated according to whim.

Once again, he'd been fed and flattered into submission, though he should have known better. Bruce had recognised him for what he was: a literary groupie and therefore easy prey. He was just another port in Bruce's growing emotional storm. Even so, he was a little bit grateful for the attention. Damn him.

It was obvious that Bruce was unwell. He had a nasty bronchial cough and a rash on his neck that could be chicken pox, or a herald of something worse. He said he'd got blood poisoning. Been bitten by a bat in Barbadoor, or somewhere like that, supposing such a place even existed. He was trying to make light of it. One would expect nothing else. Yet being ill was clearly depressing him. The accumulating clutter was simply a talisman, a psychological bulwark against dawning reality.

Oliver took out his notebook and toyed with his pencil. He wanted to get something down while the evening's images were fresh in his mind but couldn't decide whether to focus on Candy or Bruce. In a way, Bruce was more straightforward. He might write about the apartment; about how much easier it is to achieve complexity than simplicity: to produce an essay versus a poem. But something Bruce had said, while they were looking at Candy's photograph, sent him down a different path: 'You know, the more one discovers, the more one understands how everything is connected.'

Bruce was right about that. But he was quite wrong about the Mapplethorpe. Candy's face might be a mask, but her eyes told you everything. She looked as if she could bite — and enjoy biting you.

6

A friend from the scene worked below stairs, so Candy was familiar with the Hyde Park Hotel's antics and legends. But she'd never been anywhere that could match its opulence. Or its clientele. The tuxes and furs were out in force. Fashion was the new religion. Venerate Versace. Gucci is God.

The lobby was crawling with silver-haired professional gentlemen, but none of them appeared to be the one she was meeting. There were plenty of professionals among the women too. Hookers in Halston.

She'd chosen her own look for its unremarkable qualities — a Burberry trench, with a Hermès scarf tied like a cravat — though in present company she was conspicuously underdressed. She sat with her knees together and the coat pulled down to divert attention from bordello heels and a black rubber dress. She looked cool, but her blood was up.

Nine fifteen. He was late. It was his first appointment, and it was very bad form. Another five minutes and she began to wonder whether it might not have been her mistake after all. She crossed to the desk and waited while the receptionist greased up to a wizened old bird who seemed in no hurry to move.

'Thank you, Your Grace, I *do* hope you enjoy your stay', he said finally, turning away. Stuck-up little prick.

'Excuse me!' she said, realising she was invisible.

'Yes *Madam*?'

'I'm waiting for a guest of yours — Mr Diessel. He said he'd meet me in the lobby, but I think he must have forgotten. Could you please call his room?'

'With pleasure miss', he said, picking up the phone. 'Whom shall I say is waiting?'

'Candide Masters ...' Well, she wasn't about to say Mistress Candide.

'Thank you, sir — I'll tell her.' The receptionist replaced the receiver, not bothering to hide his distaste. 'He says to go up — 325 on the third floor.'

As a rule, she never went up to a client's room alone on a first appointment. She liked to meet on neutral ground, somewhere she could make her excuses and leave if she got the wrong vibe. But according to Margrét, Diessel's bona fides were impeccable — a friend-of-a-friend, a straight-up-and-down submissive. So, while her instincts said leave, his references gave him the benefit of the doubt.

Unbuttoning her coat in the lift she released the sweet, choco-latey aroma of warm rubber. God, it smelt good. If you could bottle that scent, you'd make a fortune. It was the best aphrodisiac. She rubbed her bum against the lift car wall and let the slippery material caress the back of her thighs. Only intense irritation prevented her from being aroused.

Outside Diessel's room she paused, then knocked. He must have been waiting, for the door opened immediately.

'Mistress', he said, bowing. 'Welcome ... do come in.' The voice was cultured but with a hint of menace. He wore his silver hair cropped short, and a crisp white shirt emphasised the richness of his tan. Rimless spectacles framed cool grey eyes. He could have been Heinrich Himmler, fresh from the Berghof.

The room was dark, save for the light of an altar candle, which was magnified in the mirror over the mantelpiece. Incense burned in the hearth and perfume wafted towards her: a nice touch. She removed her coat and untied her scarf, letting both fall to the floor. 'Pick them up!' she said.

'Yes Mistress; thank you Mistress.' He mimed obsequiousness, but not quite well enough.

'I believe you need to be disciplined. Is that so?'

'Yes Mistress!'

He dropped on all fours and hung his head. If he'd had a tail, he would have wagged it. She opened her bag and took out a coiled whip. 'Pull up your shirt — I want to see flesh!' Another obedient movement.

Though her eyes were still adjusting to the darkness, her hearing was sharp. From somewhere to the left came a tinkling sound, as if something small and metallic had been dropped into a basin. She spun around. 'What was that — who else is here?'

'No one, Mistress,' Diessel said, smoothly. 'I can assure you: we are quite alone.'

A door opened, its hinges complaining, but before she could move a hand pressed a wet cloth against her face. In a moment she succumbed.

* * *

Her head was spinning; her eyelids were too heavy to open. Diessel! How could she have been so stupid? Gustav Diessl played Jack the Ripper — Lulu's nemesis in *Pandora's Box*. Lulu had given herself freely to a penniless Jack and he'd returned the favour by slicing off her tits.

'She's woken up!' … Diessel's voice. A wave of pain engulfed her. She almost passed out again.

'Welcome to my final examination', said another voice, softly in her ear. 'This is where you give me marks for style and content … and then when I've finished you get to call *me* Mistress!' Margrét! The little bitch! Candy tried to get up, but movement was impossible.

She was spreadeagled on the bed, her wrists and ankles cuffed. The chill on her skin told her that her dress had been rolled up and her stockings and pants removed. She smelt blood and knew it was hers. This wasn't role-play. There was no safeword. She arched her back and pulled against the cuffs with all her strength, but it was useless.

Margrét crawled over her as if she were an assault course, bearing down on her and aggravating what felt like a thousand wasp stings on her legs. She began to cry, silently, her tears absorbed by her scarf, which they'd wound around her face. If she struggled, they'd probably dope her again, or hurt her even more. She tried to control her breathing, to stay calm, to conceal the extent of her suffering. Why give them the satisfaction?

* * *

41

A rat-a-tat at the door. Then the sound of a key in the lock; then a scream: the maid. 'Oh, Mary Mother of God! What have they done to you?'

Candy heard the girl knock over the phone, then pick up the receiver and dial: 'Get the manager up here quick … 325. There's been a murder!' Except her Irish burr gave the last word extra colour — *Morrh-dah!*

The manager's voice was more reassuring: 'What's happened here?' he asked the girl, but her response was lost beneath the sobbing. Candy sensed his clammy hand on her wrist. 'Stop crying, for heaven's sake. She's not dead!'

Genius: tell me something I don't know. He removed the scarf from her head and prised the gag from her mouth.

'And I think you, miss, had better try to explain yourself before I call the police …'

'It was a game with my boyfriend', she said, thinking on her feet, or rather not. 'We were experimenting. He's gone to get cigarettes. He'll be back soon.'

'Do you want me to leave you like this?'

'No, please, I'd prefer it if you could undo me … thank you.'

'Where's the key for these things?'

'On the mantelpiece, I think.' It was an educated guess, based on the routine in her rooms. Margrét had been well trained, at least so she believed.

'Got it.'

When they finally left her alone, she shuffled into the bathroom and turned on the shower, allowing the cold jet to play on her face and soak her hair. For a while she just stood there, holding it together. Then she loosened the buckles on her dress and let the water run beneath the rubber and down her back. Eventually she grasped the hem and peeled it over her head.

Slowly, she assessed the damage. Her ankles and wrists were chafed, her abdomen was scratched, and her fanny was sore. What had they forced inside her — a bottle? No marks for imagination. Straight from *Hollywood Babylon*. The worst thing was the zigzag

42

line of tiny cuts down the inside of both legs, which burned when she touched them. She should have them looked at. Apart from that, the only serious injury was to her pride.

She tried to piece together what had happened after they knocked her out, but there wasn't much to work with. She was sure that Diessel had wielded the scalpel, but Margrét had done most of the talking. Perhaps in hindsight, she should have guessed that something was brewing. Margrét thought she was smart. And most often she probably got away with it because other people weren't much smarter. Well not this time. Candy liked to joke that she had friends in low places, but now they'd be useful.

Looking around the room, she checked to see if they'd left anything incriminating. Not a trace. Unless you counted fingerprints, and she certainly wasn't about to summon forensics. She examined the bed, then pulled up the duvet to hide the mess. Pity the poor cleaner.

Recoiling from the thought of wearing the rubber dress again, she patted it dry and placed it in her bag with the rest of her things. Then she tied the scarf around her neck and pulled the coat belt tight. Nobody would guess she had nothing on underneath. All she needed before setting off was a fag to steady her nerves.

For a moment she considered walking home but looked at her heels and doubted they'd last five-hundred yards. A taxi was waiting in the rank, and she got in: 'Where to love?' She gave her address, but almost immediately changed her mind. Leaning forward, she tapped on the glass: 'Sorry, change of plan …'

There was a greasy spoon, not far from Kensington Palace, where she sometimes stopped off if she'd been out all night. Lady Di dropped in, now and then, for her morning cup of joe. They had a framed photograph of Di with Liborio, who basically lived behind the counter. She almost felt sorry for Di. Acting the Londoner, like sweet Marie Antoinette tending her lambkins. But if she had to confront half the crap that real Londoners dealt with every day, she'd soon change her tune.

The caff was rammed, the only free spot being right next to the kitchen. A yob in a donkey jacket had a newspaper spread out in front of him. 'Do you mind?' she said. He folded the paper to make room and she caught the headline. MINERS SHAFTED. Nice; worthy of the Toad himself. Well, they weren't alone; and fuck them in any case. Why should they expect a job for life? Any working girl could explain the dynamics of a free-market economy. She nodded to Liborio, and he came over, all smiles, wiping his hands on his apron. 'What can I get you, darlin' — the usual?'

'Uh-huh, but two eggs this morning, please. I need building up.'

'Okay, two eggs; and for you, special lady, *extra* bacon. And strong black coffee?'

'Great ... thank you!'

The smell of fresh toast was a welcome benediction. And Mastermind opposite kept his eyes fixed on the *Mirror*, which was another blessing. She took her time, lighting up again when she'd finished her coffee. God, what a mess! Right now, she needed time to reflect and to lick her wounds. Get away from it all. But the priority was damage limitation, which meant checking the appointments book for the day.

* * *

Candy switched on the light in the dressing room. No sign of Margrét, but her own things were all in order. She pulled out a few pieces at random and got dressed.

Opening the connecting door to the salon, she glanced at the mantelpiece and saw the note she'd half-expected to find. The envelope was white with black edging, of the kind the Victorians used during periods of mourning. She tore at the paper, revealing a stiff card, also edged in black. The message was penned in an elongated script. Margrét's handwriting, no question:

Scene I — mortification

Scene II — unto death

The card fell to the floor. Acid rose in her throat. She scrambled to the lavatory and vomited, retching until her diaphragm threatened to burst.

When it was over, she knelt on the tiles, exhausted, her head resting on the edge of the bath. What could she possibly have done to deserve the trials of the past twelve hours? There were some crazies in the darker bands of the spectrum, for sure, but she'd never heard of anyone being threatened with death, except in a few South American snuff flicks. And no one was sure whether they were for real. No, it was bravado. But if they were trying to scare her, they'd made a pretty good start.

The flashing light on her answering machine told her that the tape was full. She pressed the button: *Hello, my dear, are you free tonight or perhaps tomorrow?* Ugh! You've got to be kidding. The voice alone made her skin crawl. *Spitting Image* had him perfectly: the self-basting hair. They were so clever.

She fast-forwarded to the next caller: The Bully. He was one client she couldn't cope with on her own. But there was no way of finding another maid in time, unless one of the bimbos upstairs was free. Even then, she wouldn't be able to face him. Discerning in all things, he insisted on being caned on the balls of his feet. Apart from the exquisite discomfort it caused, and the precision it demanded, it was one way of ensuring his cow of a wife would never find the marks. His number was there, along with all his requirements.

'Hello…Good morning. May I to speak to Sir Terence?' she said, surprised at the tremulous quality of her own voice. 'No? Well in that case could you say that the dental surgery called and that unfortunately we're going to have to reschedule his appointment…'

Duty done, the stinging in her legs prompted one more call. She flicked open her Filofax and found the number.

'Doctor Nelson please…it's personal…Yes, I'll wait, but it is quite urgent.' Then the clunk of the receiver being set down, succeeded by low-level hospital chatter. It was an age before he picked up.

'Luke? Hi, it's Candy. I need you to bring your sewing kit over.'

'Why…what's up? You don't sound so cocky.'

'I'm all right. Can you meet me at my rooms? I really don't want to have to show myself at the hospital.'

'Okay but give me an hour. I need to finish my rounds.'

Luke was one of her oldest friends and probably the only senior registrar in the country with a penis stud and nipple rings; but then one could never be sure. He had big brown eyes and an unruly mop of black hair, which he pomaded and combed back. He was probably forty but could pass for thirty-five. With his embroidered waistcoat and silver fob watch, he looked every bit the Edwardian dandy. Distinguished, but devilish. Plus, he was a switch, which made him a popular guest at every party.

'You've been in the wars', Luke said, when she showed him her legs. 'What on earth happened?'

'A little skirmish, that's all.'

'Do you want to tell me about it?'

'No. It wasn't planned, but it's nothing to worry about.'

'Some of these cuts will need sutures — they're quite deep.'

'I guessed so … that's why I called you.'

'What else do I need to look at?'

'My bladder hurts, but I've managed to pee, so I don't think anything's ruptured.'

'What did he push up there … I'm assuming it was he?'

'It felt like a champagne bottle. I couldn't tell you the exact vintage.'

'So Fatty Arbuckle strikes again', he said. 'I thought mothers warned nice girls not to play with men like that.'

'Yes, well I'm not such a nice girl. And anyway, I fell into his trap.'

'That doesn't sound like you.'

'I know. But don't worry, it won't happen again. I'm going to put a hex on him.'

Luke bathed the cuts with a pungent fluid, which made her almost leap out of her skin, and put neat little stitches in the deeper ones. He said to keep them uncovered for at least a fortnight to encourage the healing process. But how was she meant to do that? Her legs looked like a Frankenstein experiment, as if they'd been opened and de-boned. If she wanted to scare business away, parading them in front of everyone was a great way to go about it.

Facing the inevitable, she opened the diary again and rang the next number. She had to admit to a grudging admiration for Margrét. Her attention to detail was exemplary. Every client for the next three weeks was documented thoroughly, including their safeword and the code name or phrase that was to be used in case they had to be contacted. After that the diary was blank. When she was done, she closed the book and put it back in the safe. Then she kicked off her shoes and stretched out on the sofa.

She woke up shivering. The windows were wide open, the temperature had dropped, and the failing light had cast the room back into darkness. For the first time in her life, she began to feel sorry for herself and knew it could be a precipitous path. Time to go home.

7

Candy's Filofax contained her life's work. The names she'd gathered ran the gamut from the great and the good to the downright disreputable, from the famed and the titled to the deservedly obscure. The only common factor was a significant kink of some kind. In the right hands, with the wrong motive, the information would be dynamite.

She looked up a number she'd dialled only once before. When they'd first met, George Holloway had been a chief superintendent in the Flying Squad. He'd retired shortly before a major bribery scandal broke. Strange, but she'd met more coppers on the scene than almost any other profession. Might as well have joined the Freemasons. Now George worked for what he called an 'intelligence-based' security firm (police intelligence — an obvious oxymoron), helping companies to snoop on their unsuspecting staff. He was habitually discreet, good at covering his tracks, and not averse to operating slightly 'outside the box' as he put it. 'Bent' would have been generous.

'All right, let's see if you can track down Bonnie and Clyde', she said, picking up the phone.

'*Cherchez la femme, pardieu! Cherchez la femme!*' said George. He rated himself as a bit of a linguist. He was probably right though. 'I need her full name and as much background as you can fill in.'

'She's called Margrét Lindgren, from Copenhagen. Blonde hair, blue eyes; about five-eight; and I guess nineteen or twenty. She's kinky and she used to be my maid and sleep in my dressing room. That's really all I know.'

'Any defining marks?'

'She has a couple of tattoos. There could be more, but I've never seen her completely naked.' Candy gave him the details.

'What did she do in the evenings?'

'Well, I met her at Der Putsch, but that was it … just the once. I don't know where else she went. Our paths never crossed outside of work, and I only ever saw her in the afternoons unless we had a special client to look after. Then we'd work late. Occasionally all night.'

'How often was that?'

'Maybe twice a month. Some of my clients are particularly demanding.'

'What sort of thing?'

'None of your business. Use your imagination!' she said, sensing that it was already in overdrive.

'Did you ever get the feeling that she was unhappy with the arrangement?'

'No, it suited both of us very well.'

'You don't think she might have been jealous of you, the powerful über-domme?'

'Look, I'm beginning to think I ought to be charging you, not the other way round. I've told you all I know. Go find them!'

For the next few days, Candy barely left the house, other than to buy groceries. She knew that the best way to stave off depression was to keep busy. A lapsed, though not unaccomplished cook, she began to enjoy the discipline of preparing regular meals; and for the first time in her life, she tended a well-stocked fridge.

Home was in a Victorian mews that had once provided stabling for a terrace on the northern edge of Hyde Park. The property was much the same as it had been built, with double doors opening onto a garage on the ground floor and living accommodation above.

The flat was just a living room, with a galley kitchen, and a bedroom with a connecting bathroom. She didn't have much stuff. A radiogram in the living room sat next to a long line of albums, organised according to the date she'd acquired them. So, Bowie sat next to Brahms, and *Rubber Soul* next to *Sticky Fingers*, a juxtaposition she particularly enjoyed. A bowl of flowers — today white anemones — sat on the marble-topped dining table. There was a TV, of course, and a Habitat sofa, and that was about it.

The only concessions to art or personal history were two photographs that hung in the bedroom. The first was from a series that Bob Carlos Clarke had shot for Daniel James, who'd made the rubber dress she was wearing in the picture. She'd donned a black wig for the shoot, styled in a Cleopatra cut, and looked suitably aloof. When Bob showed her the contacts a couple of days later, she got very excited and said he should call the picture *Mighty Aphrodite*, but instead he called it *Auto-Dom*.

Bob might have been man material. She'd wanted him to hit on her, just so she could mess with his head, but he never did. Silly boy couldn't take a hint.

The other photograph was a portrait, a Punk take on a classical pose, in which her hands cupped her naked breasts. One eye was closed in a suggestive wink. The picture was a gift from Alice Man, who'd taken the photograph for the cover of *i-D* magazine. Alice said it made her look like Agrippina, Caligula's sister. Not a bad start, really, for a dom.

Her one indulgence was her car — a pagoda-roof Mercedes — which she kept tucked up in the garage. She'd inherited the Merc when it was fifteen years old and had cosseted it ever since. It was white with olive green leather, and she loved it. Speeding along an open road, listening to the sweet sound of the engine and the contented burble of the exhaust, was pure heaven.

On the second Sunday after what Luke called her 'epiphany', she got up early and set off for the sticks to see Bella, her sister. It was a crisp autumnal morning and she drove with the roof down and the heater full on, a cashmere scarf wrapped around her head.

Heading east, she confronted a scrappy landscape that she'd watched change over time and gradually come to hate. An ancient tapestry of fields and hedgerows was being divvied up and auctioned off to a relentless horde of New Town speculators. The countryside of her childhood had gone. Soon there would be no memories left.

Although she recoiled from the stuffiness of her sister's life in the country, and the smell of dogs and Barbour jackets that greeted her in the hallway, she found the rituals of Sunday lunch strangely comforting. It was one of the few things that kept her going there. That, and the prospect of seeing Lucy, her niece.

Lucy was a kindred spirit: a heartbreaker in the making, a little love bomb. Uncorrupted by the world, she didn't register skin colour, or wealth, or class, or sexual orientation, she simply noted who was kind and who was not, who had time for her, and who made her laugh or cry. Candy and Lucy adored one another. But part way there, Candy realised her mistake. She should have worn a long skirt, but she was so used to flashing her pins that it hadn't occurred to her. What do you say to a three-year-old kid when she asks: 'Aunty Catherine, why do your legs look all funny?' And how do you admit to your little sister that you spent the night with a psychopath whose idea of entertainment was to torment you half to death?

It would be hard enough trying to explain that to Bella, but her brother-in-law was such a dick, he'd probably have a fit. He'd go blabbing to her parents. Next thing her father would be on the phone, creating a drama, telling her she was making her mother ill again. Her visit would cause more anxiety than she could handle. She'd been crazy even to have considered going. She would just have to stop and find a phone box.

Slowing at the turn off, she looked in the mirror to see a red BMW, headlights flashing, closing in fast. Another banker boy heading home. The imbecile waited until he was no more than a car's length away before swinging out violently, horn blaring, tyres squealing. She flipped the bird. 'Fucking oik!' God, how she loathed Essex.

* * *

On the Friday after her abortive road trip, Luke came to remove her stitches. She'd planned to meet him in her rooms but changed her mind at the last minute. It was cold out, and getting dark, and she couldn't face going there alone. Only a handful of people had ever visited her at home. It wasn't that she was reclusive. At least not entirely. But she guarded her privacy. Luke was a special case though, so the usual rules didn't apply.

'You're making good progress', he said, running his fingertips lightly over her wounds. 'If you're lucky, the scarring should be quite light, though it will never disappear altogether.'

'I hope so. But I suppose it could be worse — at least they're not on the back of my legs.'

'Don't tell me you never let anyone see the inside of your lovely thighs … that would be a terrible waste.'

His fingers paused for effect, and she shuddered. Oh, please God, don't let him stop.

'Are you getting fresh with me?'

'The idea had crossed my mind.'

'Be careful. I'm like the black widow spider. I like to consume my lovers.'

'During or afterwards?'

'I like to start from the beginning. It's more interesting that way. You know the rule — no pain, no gain.'

'I'm willing to offer myself up for sacrifice', he said, 'If it will help cheer you up.'

'You know, it just might.'

8

Oliver caught himself looking out of the window. Normally, Candy passed between five and five-thirty in the afternoon. Mostly she'd wave and keep going. Occasionally she'd cross the street and buzz the doorbell. He could tell whether she was going to stop or not by the tempo of her walk. She came for what she called her 'culture shot'. He'd tell her about books he was reading or exhibitions he'd seen; she'd mostly talk about music or clubs.

Each time he tried to tease a little more information out of her, but she was so effortlessly evasive that one day he'd given up coaxing and asked her straight: 'So how do you go about satisfying someone you've never met before?'

She shrugged: 'Basically it comes down to acting ability.'

'What do you mean?'

'Well, first you have to work out who the guy wants you to be — the sort of woman he fantasises about — and then you have to get into the role.'

'But how do you do that?'

'Sometimes they tell you beforehand. If not, you pick up on body language. You look for clues.'

'You mean it's psychological as well as physical?'

'Kind of. It's a bit like being a silent movie star. There's a storyline but no script.' She tilted her head and fluttered her eyelids. '*We didn't need dialogue ... we had faces!*' She had Norma Desmond perfectly: the manic eyes, the mean mouth, the thin lips. It was uncanny.

Before he knew it, she'd diverted his attention and was talking about Louise Brooks. He was ashamed to admit that he'd seen none of her films.

'But you must know *Pandora's Box*?' she asked. 'It's where Lulu comes from. Lulu loves sex. Lots of sex. So obviously she's a bad girl.'

'That sounds familiar', he said, and Candy responded with her wonderful cackle.

'The amazing thing is how radiant Lulu is on screen. She's lit up like a lighthouse. No prizes for guessing what she's been up to.' Candy's expression suggested he'd committed some unknown crime. 'But you sort of know it won't end well. It's a man's world after all.'

Strange how you can recall entire conversations and yet forget whole periods of your life.

No sign of Candy. That made three weeks in a row. Perhaps she'd gone on holiday. Even tarts must take time off. The last time she called, she'd left a video of *Pandora's Box*. It had been sitting in front of him, on the desk, ever since, Lulu's sweet face silently reproachful.

'Okay Lulu, I give in. I'll watch your lousy movie.' With whisky and cigarettes to hand, he popped the cassette into the machine and pressed 'play'.

October 1984

9

Oliver awoke to news of the bomb on the radio. Disbelieving at first, he got up and turned on the little portable television at the foot of the bed.

A savage tear in the facade of the Grand Hotel stood out ominously dark against the illuminated stucco; a half-clothed victim was being hoisted slowly from the debris. The camera zoomed in to show the old boy grimacing with pain, struggling to preserve his modesty. Jesus, he couldn't bear to watch. And then the realisation struck. Holly and Henry Pound were staying in the hotel!

He dialled his parents' number automatically. His father picked up after one ring: 'If you're calling to ask about your sister, she's fine', he said. 'But she has no idea what's happened to Henry. He wasn't in bed with *her*. And nobody seems to know where he *is*. She says it's not the first time he hasn't come home ...'

So, they'd finally pulled it off. He began to see what Mrs T meant when she spoke of 'the enemy within'. There was revolution in the air.

He knew what it was like to be on the receiving end of the IRA's largesse: the blizzard of glass, the terrible silence, then the sirens sounding to eternity. It had been an everyday Knightsbridge scene — Christmas shoppers and families and traffic, quietly going about their business. Next thing, he was on the ground, his eyes and mouth clogged with filth. He had no idea how long he lay there: minutes, hours? Eventually, someone helped him up: 'You all right sir? You had a lucky escape!'

They'd tried to put him in an ambulance, but all he'd wanted to do was go home and run a bath. Before that, he'd never dwelt on death, certainly not his own. Now he was aware of its random grasp, he was more watchful.

He dressed quickly and went down to the newsagent. As he expected, the papers had gone to press before news of the bomb reached the world. The *Telegraph* headline was SIX DIE IN RAIL CRASH. The country's entire infrastructure was disintegrating. But there at the bottom of the front page was a late news item:

BOMB BLAST AT THATCHER HOTEL. No more than a dozen lines, it read as if it had been phoned in drunkenly to the night desk and gone straight to press. He had a piece of his own to hand in, but it was obvious that the whole of Saturday's edition would be recast. May as well deliver it anyway.

Over breakfast he turned to the arts pages to find a review of Michael Radford's *1984*. He'd seen the movie and not thought much of it, but then it was hard to convey the elemental chill of Orwell's text. How had it been pitched in Hollywood: dystopian future love story? No. Lone hero versus totalitarian state — more likely. Mostly it was about betrayal, but then that's a much harder sell.

What really interested him was Richard Burton as O'Brien. It was Burton's last role, shot in the final few months of his life. There was a poignancy in seeing him on screen, still vigorous. It was the same with Clark Gable in *The Misfits*. History told you that time was running out for them. Had indeed run out. But seeing them, you couldn't quite believe it.

Watching Mrs T on television, opening the Conservative Party conference precisely on schedule, provoked the opposite reaction. The bomb had her name on it. She shouldn't have survived, but there she was, not a hair out of place. Magnificent in a bloodless kind of way.

Still, the Provos were right: *'Today we were unlucky, but remember we only have to be lucky once. You will have to be lucky always.'*

* * *

Fleet Street was really just a myth. Only a handful of papers had been based there and most of them were long gone. But it was through myths such as this that the press imagined itself and on which it thrived. Of the papers that remained, the *Telegraph* was the grandest and would most likely be the last.

Usually at this hour the *Telegraph* building was like a great ocean liner lying idly at its berth, its vast halls empty, its turbines slowly raising steam far below. But the second Oliver pushed the lift button, he registered a buzz of nervous energy. Up on the first floor he poked his nose into the newsroom and sniffed. You could always gauge the level of activity by the density of the cigarette smoke. Definitely at the upper end of the scale.

Turning round, he bumped into the rangy figure that was Bill Deedes. Bill was one of those constantly cheerful people who seem to make industry effortless, and for whom editing the paper fleshed out the day between luncheon and dinner. What was it Oscar Wilde said? Work: the curse of the drinking classes. That was Bill, always a couple of gins under par. But he was nobody's fool. Like Reagan, he played the age card well. It was a class act.

'Oh, hello Bill ... quite a night!'

'Certainly eventful, dear boy. Never imagined they'd stoop so low.'

'I saw Mrs T on television before I left the flat. You have to admire her. She was cool as they come.'

'I think we've witnessed a transformation', said Bill. 'Shurely less *Iron Lady*, more *Woman of Shteel*.' Was it his lisp, or his waggery? When Bill said it, it came out as *Ironing Lady* which summed her up perfectly.

'And what brings you to this benighted land?' Bill asked. Although he shot the familiar smile, his eyes lacked their usual sparkle.

'I've got a piece to hand in, so I dropped by.'

'Sorry old son, we're going to have to pass on the arts this weekend. We're filling her up with news.'

'I guessed that might happen ... if you can't hold it over, perhaps I can get the *Architectural Review* to run it.'

'Good idea', said Bill. 'Never let a good piece go to waste. Now if you'll excuse me, I must make myself useful.'

Back at his desk that evening, Oliver sat working his way through his notes. In journalism, recycling was a way of life. He still had material he hadn't been able to use. The piece could do with being a bit longer. Or maybe it should be shorter. Then again, perhaps he should leave it alone.

A light came on in the hotel opposite. The peep show was about to begin, but it was too banal, and he wasn't in the mood.

He switched on the hi-fi and turned up the volume. Nina Simone's voice emerged, reassuringly rich and smoky as old bourbon. He admired her morality and envied her generosity. What does it take, to lay yourself on the line for others, as she had done?

Completely bewitched by Lulu, he'd watched *Pandora's Box* over and over. He'd even tried to persuade the *Telegraph* to send him to Upstate New York to interview Louise Brooks, though in old age she'd become famously reclusive. And on each viewing, he'd wondered why Candy hadn't come back to collect the tape, as arranged.

Though he missed Candy, it hadn't occurred to him to try to contact her. Typically, he was passive. He weighed, he reckoned, but he never reached out, or made the first move. At school he'd been known as 'Sheep', as in 'Sheep in Woolf's clothing', and like all caricatures it contained an element of truth. Well, if the day's events offered a lesson, it was 'do it now'. He picked up his coat and let Nina's free spirit guide him to the door.

10

The alleyway was unswept and empty, save for a slack figure standing in the shadows. Opening the car door, Oliver battled the stink of urine and wet newsprint. Walking briskly, he turned east, past a decaying terrace where moments of Georgian grandeur shone through the grime. An illuminated sign advertised *Private Tuition — En français*. A malnourished girl in silver hotpants lounged in the doorway, beginning her lonely shift. '*Parlez-vous* handsome … looking for company?' She tried to take his arm, but he sidestepped her on the narrow pavement, dropping one foot in the gutter. 'No thank you. Not tonight.'

He was more familiar with Soho in the mornings, shopping in Berwick Street or Lina Stores. Now the market was deserted, and the path was slippery underfoot. He picked his way through the debris until a narrow court led him into a gaudy world of neon lights and blind shop fronts, where almost anything illicit might be bought, above or below the counter.

On Shaftesbury Avenue he found what he was looking for: a wide doorway beneath a garish halo of neon sweet jars. Hard to miss. For the avoidance of doubt, a brass plate announced *Bon-Bon: Members Only*.

The club was one of Candy's rendezvous. It was one of the few pieces of information he'd managed to coax from her, though he had no idea whether it was still part of her routine. One way to find out. Why page the Oracle when you can ask a barman!

What little charm the old ballroom once possessed had long faded. Velvet curtains screened the remains of a stage, and a grand piano sat forlornly in one corner. Mirrored walls magnified the room's dreariness almost to infinity. The music at least retained some glamour. Ella Fitzgerald's rendition of *Lullaby of Birdland* flowed silkily through the room.

In the Sixties, the club had been famous for the starriness of its cabaret and the loucheness of its clientele. It was one of the places that made London swing. As if in flashback, he had an image of how the room must have been in its prime. Aristocrats, East-End gangsters, and television personalities rubbing shoulders. The men in black tie, or white if they'd come on from a ball; girlfriends in gowns; the hostesses in mini dresses serving martinis and high-balls, picking up trade along the way; a cigarette girl working the tables in a similar manner; crisp notes being pulled from money clips; assignations arranged. Their ghosts roamed.

He pulled up a stool at the end of the bar and opened a new pack of Marlboro. His hands were unsteady. First-night nerves? Or maybe the lingering shock of the membership fee they'd extorted at the door. It was going to be an expensive night. 'Whisky please … Macallan if you have it.' The barman looked at him pityingly and offered a light.

'I'm looking for a girl …' he continued.

'Then you've come to the right place', said the little fellah, deadpan.

Very droll. The guy obviously fancied himself. In fact, on second viewing he could have passed for Robert De Niro. That is if De Niro ever had his legs sawn off.

'She's called Candy ...'

'Sorry, I dunno her. I'm new here. Just coverin' for my cousin. Alfredo's gone back to Sicily for a funeral ... if you know what I mean. You wanna chat, you gotta talk to one of the girls. House rules.' He gestured in the direction of a tall brunette, who slid her glass along the bar. 'Ask Nola ... she knows everyone here.'

'Hello, er ... I'm Oliver', he offered. 'Will you have a drink?' The abbreviated barman filled her glass, then retreated. He was discreet at least, our Robert De Zero.

'And a cigarette?'

'Thanks, but I only smoke French.'

'I'm looking for a friend', he said. 'I think she comes in occasionally.'

'Really, what's her name?'

'She calls herself Candy ...'

'How sweet.'

'Like Candy Darling.'

'And then a little sour.'

'I asked the barman, but he said he didn't know her. I think he's playing dumb.'

'Not playing darling. He's as dumb as they come. We're counting the days until Alfredo gets back. Can't stop the little creep pestering the girls for favours. He's hung like a Chihuahua, but still can't keep it in his pants.'

She took a sip of champagne and placed the glass on the bar. 'I'm sorry, I digress. What does your friend look like?'

'About your height, I guess. Her hair's platinum blonde, cut short. And she has emerald-green eyes. Quite hard to forget.'

Hers were memorable too. Pale blue, flecked with purple, like tiny cornflowers. She looked as if she was trying to retrieve some long-lost detail: 'I do know her. She comes in but doesn't work here. I haven't seen her in a while though.' She paused, turning her glass slowly. 'What's your connection?' she asked finally, 'You're not a copper?'

'No! Nothing like that! But it's a long story ...'

'Tell me anyway. I have all evening.'

She guided him to a table, where a bottle of Moët was already on ice, and launched into what he guessed was a familiar routine, the subject matter based on comforting generalities. They talked about the weather, holiday plans, and the history of the club. She kept the conversation moving along but gave little away.

When the second bottle arrived, she unwound noticeably. She was obviously earning her keep. He gave her a potted version of his Candy story, keeping close to the truth this time, and she seemed attentive enough.

'And you, how long have you known her?' he asked.

To his surprise, she sprang straight back with an answer.

'I met her at the Windmill, a few years ago. At *La Vie en Rose*. She was in the chorus line to begin with. Then she developed a burlesque routine and Paul Raymond gave her a slot of her own. She was a bit of a star.'

'Were you a dancer too?'

'Heavens, no! I was a hostess.'

'Is that better or worse?'

'That depends, darling. It's certainly easier on your knees.' She paused, as if waiting for him to laugh, but he was obviously missing the joke.

'Why *La Vie en Rose*?'

'I got fired from the Playboy Club. I needed a job.'

'Strange, I was just thinking about that place.' One of his father's high-roller friends took them there one evening. After dinner they'd gone to the tables, where they witnessed scenes of almost Roman decadence. Men happily dropped sums he'd have struggled to make in a year: probably ten years. And the Bunnies, with their extravagantly long legs, were attentive but only really turned on the charm if you rolled very high indeed.

'You mean you were a Bunny?'

'Yes, I was Bunny Nola for six months.'

'I would like to have seen that. You must have looked very fetching in that costume.'

'I believe I did.'

'So why didn't it last?'

'I committed the cardinal sin. I went home with a Keyholder.'

'You mean a punter?'

'Yes — a Moroccan guy. They used to get a lot of Arabs in, and they were big spenders. They liked to shed it by the ton. Especially if you were blonde.'

'So did you dye your hair?'

'No, I didn't, but a lot of girls did. I wouldn't have touched most of the guys with a ten-foot pole. I preferred to look after the *gentlemen*. Some of the regulars were lovely. George Best and Peter Sellers were my favourites, my boys. George is a darling and Peter always tucked a twenty into my cuff when I served him. He told me a joke once; do you want to hear it?'

'Go on …'

'A Jewish guy phones home: *Hello?*

Hi mom, it's Ruben. How are you?

Fabulous darling and how lovely to hear from you!

Sorry, wrong number, he says, and hangs up.'

'Very droll. Sellers was there the night I went. He looked cadaverous. So, what happened with the Moroccan?'

'Well, this guy had been pestering me for ages and secretly I rather fancied him. He reminded me of Omar Sharif. But it was against the rules. I think they were terrified they'd get busted for prostitution. Nobody was even allowed to touch the girls. Except Victor and Hef, that is. They basically had proprietors' rights.'

'So how did they find out?'

'They used to spy on us. They wanted you to think they were your best friend, but they were quite creepy. The doorman told Victor he'd seen me get into this guy's Maserati and that was it — ex-Bunny Nola.'

'Serves them right they got shut down', said Oliver, refilling her glass.

Midnight had passed, and those delicate blue eyes were losing their dazzle. The second bottle was half full and set to remain that way. Nola was flagging. 'It doesn't look as if your friend's coming in tonight', she said.

He nodded to the waiter and the bill arrived. He didn't bother to check it, just tossed his Amex onto the tray. What the hell. When he got up to leave, she offered her card. On it was embossed her name and number. 'Phone me if you like', she said. 'You'll get my machine, but don't be put off.'

11

Mondays were usually idle. It was a day without deadlines and thus an opportunity to lie in and recover from the exertions of the weekend. Oliver awoke unusually late, even so. Not hungover exactly, but groggy. He got up and rang Jan, hoping he'd be free later, ready for a progress report, but there was no reply. He switched on the radio, in anticipation of Robin Day and *The World at One*. Then came the ritual of a coffee and a smoke, and the prospect of another day spent alone.

Nola had mentioned a club called Maitresse, where she said Candy liked to go: 'And who knows, you might enjoy it. Perhaps I'll see you there?' He hadn't taken her seriously. 'Maybe', he'd said, which as any student of English usage knows means *absolutely not*. But the prospect of Nola's company was enough of a draw. The memory of her wrapped in slippery satin brought an immediate tumescence, though another part of him shrank. Unable to make up his mind, he lit another cigarette and waited for the decision to make itself.

Maitresse had opened at the beginning of the year, and he vaguely recalled reading about it in *Time Out*. Nola had said simply that there was a dress code and smiled. He had a pretty good idea what she meant, but his wardrobe was never going to offer much help. He settled for black Levi's and a T-shirt, and his old leather jacket, hoping that he would at least be allowed in.

The jacket was a period piece, a Schott Perfecto, a relic from his Cambridge motorcycling days, when he'd blatted around the Fens on his father's old Norton. Posing in front of the hall mirror, he imagined a young Brando: as if. He walked the three hundred yards to the Underground with hands in pockets, shoulders hunched, getting into character.

Alighting from the train at Tottenham Court Road, he was alarmed to find the platform walls covered with a gaudy mosaic. The heavy hand was unmistakable; and there was more. Eduardo Paolozzi's artless monster pursued him right to the top of the escalators, and he hurried ahead, as if to shake him off.

Out in the street he waited at the kerb for the lights to change. It was a place he knew well. He came to rummage in the antiquarian bookshops, when he was stuck for an idea, or browse in Foyles, where it was easier to steal the books than go through the arcane ritual of paying. But tonight, everything seemed new and strange. Maybe Paolozzi's monster was an omen.

Behind the old Astoria he entered a dimly lit alleyway, which disoriented him further. A gleaming Citroën DS with French plates heralded knots of shiny clubbers; intimidating creatures who flanked the club doorway like mythical guardians of the gate. They ignored him, and he entered a lobby finished floor-to-ceiling in blood-red lacquer.

He waited his turn in front of an anaemic girl who sat at a table, taking money. It might have been her blood they'd drained to make the paint.

'Member?' she asked, not looking up.

'Er, no ... that is not yet.'

'Seven pounds then', she responded, holding out a gloved hand. Her fingernails had cut through the latex, revealing tiny shards of plum varnish, the same shade as her lipstick. 'Follow the music', she said, and he fell in with the exotic tribe on the stairs.

I give you all a girl could give you, take my tears and that's not nearly all ... Gloria Jones' hyper-energised voice bullied its way around the room, agitating the veil of smoke that hung in the air until it too seemed to dance.

The cocktail of tobacco and dope was familiar, but there was an intriguing undertow that he couldn't place. All around moved creatures of every age, shape and, he supposed, inclination. Some were cocooned and lustrous. Others wore less and were physically more fluent. A few were hooded and sinister. Against this current of forms and faces, swam tropical fish in tanks that glowed electric blue.

A languorous figure drifted past, the tang of patchouli floating in her wake. Behind her on a chain bobbed a frail-looking penitent with fresh weals across his narrow back. What had Philip Larkin said? That bending someone to your will is the very stuff of sex.

The penitent made eye contact. Jesus Christ! It was Henry Pound! But no, it couldn't be. He was in hospital, in a coma, having been pulled half-dead from the debris of the Grand Hotel. They'd found him coupled to the body of a *Guardian* journalist, surely the ultimate indignity for a Tory MP, even in Brighton. God only knows how they separated them.

Next to the bar, two girls gyrated slowly, apparently oblivious to the music. One had her hair pulled back and her fringe cut straight — a perfect datum above almond eyes. She glanced at him and turned away. The other girl moved dreamily, heavy silver earrings bumping against her slender neck. She wore a stole cape over a long rubber corset dress, which pulled in her waist and hobbled her legs. The girls exchanged a look and giggled.

'You look lost', said the one in the sheath dress.

'Hello, I'm Oliver … Oliver Woolf', he said, almost shouting to be heard.

'Like the Big Bad Wolf?'

'Ha ha … I'm afraid not.'

'A pity. I've been looking for someone like you to gobble me up.'

He laughed again, nervously. 'Can I get you a drink?'

'We don't drink', she said. 'I'm Liza, this is Alice. I haven't seen you here before, have I?'

'No, it's my first time. Are you regulars?' His awkwardness was painful, even to himself.

'Our friends run the club', she said. 'We're always here.' She spoke with a no-nonsense Lancashire accent, which suited her somehow.

'Then maybe you know my friend Candy … I hoped I might see her tonight.'

'Sure, I know Candy. I've made a few pieces for her. She's cool … not afraid to tell you what she wants.'

'Oh, and what does she want?'

'To feel strong as a woman, of course; to be empowered. Dressing up is a way of changing how you feel about yourself.'

Alice glowered: 'You're not a journalist, are you? We get your sort in here all the time, snooping about, asking questions. I can have you thrown out if I want.'

'No, you've got the wrong idea. A girl called Nola suggested I come. I met her in a nightclub. I rather hoped to find her here too.'

'You mean Nola Marks?' said Alice, 'You don't look her type. She has boys like you two at a time.'

Liza giggled, 'Yeah, and spits out the pips!'

'So, what's the deal?'

'Well, I am a writer, but I'm not looking for a story. Honestly. I came because I thought I'd find Candy.'

'A writer?' asked Liza, 'You mean a novelist?'

'Not yet … I write about architecture and art mostly, but also about film and opera. I'm a bit of a jack of all trades.'

'Oh, I see. You know, you shouldn't put yourself down.'

'No, leave that to the professionals', said Alice.

'Candy's usually here. She's been part of the scene forever, long before we started the club', Liza continued. 'But how do you know her? You don't look her sort either.'

'We're just friends. We met by chance, a couple of months ago. I used to see quite a lot of her. But I haven't heard from her for a while, and I want to be sure she's okay.'

'Are you the writer who rescued Candy from the rain?' asked Alice, now noticeably less glacial.

'Yes … she told you about that?'

'A little bit. I think she approves of you.' For a fraction of a second, he glimpsed a smile.

'Well, that's encouraging. 'I'm rather fond of her too.'

'She hasn't been in for a few weeks', said Liza. 'And if she comes in tonight, it won't be before midnight. She's usually tied up till then.'

'Or tying someone else up', said Alice.

Liza was suddenly his new best friend, his guide in the Underworld. She introduced some of her friends, male and female, though it wasn't always easy to tell which was which. Most appeared to like the fact that it was his first time.

Only Alice maintained her guard. He'd given up on her, when someone mentioned that she was Alice Man *the* photographer, as if he should have heard of her. In fact, everyone he met demanded a definite article: Liza Gray, *the* latex couturier, or Tim so-and-so *the* magazine publisher, or Peter what's-his-face *the* graphic designer. When he bumped into Alice again, he asked her about her work.

'I like to shoot people from the scene', she said. 'Candy was one of my first. She's a natural; she has no inhibitions … in any sense.'

'Do you ever show your pictures?'

'That's how I make a living, honey', she fired back, looking at him as if he were an idiot.

'I'm sorry, what I meant was, would you show them to me? I'd really like to see what you do.'

'Sure. If you want, you can come to the studio.'

'Thank you. I'd like that very much.'

There was no sign of Candy, but then he hadn't really held out much hope. Nola was a no-show too, which was the greater disappointment. He would have paid good money to see the expression on her face. When he said goodnight, Liza kissed him full on the mouth, her tongue stud clicking enthusiastically. 'If you're thinking about coming again', she said, 'you'd better let me make you something to wear.'

On the way out he passed the Citroën again. Now he knew the owners, a French couple who drove over from Paris once a month. They were intimidating in their leathers and make-up, but like others he'd got to know that evening they weren't terrifying at all; they just had no hang-ups about exploring their kinks and fetishes. He was beginning to like this strange new world. Nola may have been right. It had stirred something within him.

After the cosseting warmth of the club, the cold night air forced its way rudely into his lungs. He coughed up a gobbet of phlegm and shot it into the gutter. Too much whisky and too little dinner, not so smart in retrospect. He set a course for Bar Italia, in pursuit of a sandwich and an espresso.

They were replaying a Torino versus Juventus match on the TV when he got there; Torino was a goal up and all eyes were fixed on the screen. The redhead who served him was as brusque as ever. She shoved a cup across the counter and turned back to the match.

As he nursed his coffee, he contemplated the prospect of a date with Nola. Nola Marks, *the* nightclub hostess. He remembered her card, which he'd tucked under the corner of the typewriter, and resolved to call her.

12

Nola was essentially nocturnal, which had turned her dining habits topsy-turvy. She'd summoned Oliver to breakfast. Not his favourite meal, and certainly not his best time of day.

The last of the dawn lapped around him as he walked; a listless breeze carried leaves up from the park and he scuffed them underfoot. It was unreasonably early and far too cold to be out. At Lancaster Gate Tube, he bought a copy of the *Times* and waited for the lift.

As the train rolled on, he half read the paper. He only bought it for the obituaries. It was morbid, he knew, but he liked to see who hadn't made it through the night. The morning's selection didn't disappoint: a humble lieutenant, who'd been an unwitting hero at Passchendaele, and the titled founder of a motorcar business, both dead from decrepitude; and then François Truffaut at fifty-two of a brain tumour. Never sure what to make of Truffaut or French cinema generally, his command of the language wasn't fluent enough to gauge the nuances of the dialogue, and he mistrusted subtitles; he was fascinated though by Truffaut's transition from critic to *auteur* — a move he harboured for himself.

At the Cambridge film club, they'd shown *Jules et Jim* back-to-back with *Les Deux Anglaises et le Continent*, as a sort of yin and yang. He'd enjoyed the story of the man entangled with two sisters and it amused him how the French always cast anything *exotique* as English and vice versa. He was so engrossed in Truffaut's story, itself the stuff of cinematic legend, that he nearly missed his stop, just making it onto the platform at Farringdon as the doors slid shut.

The café was tucked away in a half-forgotten courtyard. Behind its plate-glass window it was a perfectly preserved Art Deco relic, with marble walls and a bilious terrazzo floor. Ancient ceiling fans spun above a landscape of gingham tablecloths and tubular steel furniture. Starched waitresses in yet stiffer aprons patrolled the room. Half-close your eyes, and it could have been a scene from *Picture Post*. Bert Hardy probably ate there.

As instructed, he arrived at seven; and as expected there was no sign of her. He found a seat at a corner table and ordered a coffee. The Smithfield porters ate noisily, ribbing and joshing one another. Their smocks and boots were scuffed red, and the raw smell of the market prowled beneath the familiar aroma of bacon and coffee. He took a cigarette and rolled it contemplatively between finger and thumb before lighting up.

'I'm waiting for a friend', he explained when the waitress came to take his order. 'I don't suppose she'll be long.' He'd ordered another coffee and was about to light up for the third time when all eyes suddenly turned towards the door. The collective intake of breath was palpable.

The first thing that registered was her perfume, which darted through the air. Beneath her mink, which she wore unbuttoned, her leather skirt stopped level with her stocking tops, and her shirt revealed fractionally too much breast. She was ferociously attractive, like a sleek cat of some kind. Before he could stand, she had pounced, seating herself opposite him.

'Well, you certainly know how to silence a room.'

'I do hope so', she said, then picking up the menu: 'I'm ravenous!'

She sloughed off the fur, letting it drape over the back of the chair. 'I wasn't sure what to wear. But I had a hunch the Parisian courtesan look would appeal to a nice English boy like you.'

'I'm honoured. I'd have called you sooner had I known it would be such an event.'

He noted the sharp look of disapproval from the waitress. As if in reply, Nola pulled a hip flask from her bag and poured a slug of brandy into a glass. 'I love the smell of cognac in the morning', she said, and knocked it back in one go. He laughed obediently.

They both ordered steak and eggs and he asked for a Bloody Mary, to which he added an extra dash of Tabasco. As they ate, the café began to empty, though not as quickly as it would surely have done had she not been there. Her audience was attentive, and he was privileged indeed to be seated in the front row.

* * *

After the excitement of the café, Oliver's private world seemed cramped and inhospitable. He was almost overwhelmed by the urge to call Nola, to tell her how much he'd enjoyed her company and to ask if he could see her again, but he knew that by now she would be asleep.

They'd talked for an hour, and by the end he was exhausted. She had quizzed him, gradually getting closer to home. She wanted to know where he worked — the *Telegraph*; where he lived — Bayswater; his age — the wrong side of thirty; whether he was married — no; and whether he had a girlfriend — to which he answered 'no' again. She didn't ask what he did for sex, but she was heading there.

He'd met with that line of questioning before. Asked for the umpteenth time at Holly's wedding when he was going to give up his gay bachelor life, he'd scandalised his mother by quoting advice given to Ian Fleming as a youth: 'Spend your money however you like, but never buy anything that eats.' When he told Nola she laughed so much he was afraid she would choke.

He hadn't told her everything, obviously. Mostly because it was far less interesting than she would have expected of him, but also because he hated talking about himself. The truth was he preferred to be alone. The lone Woolf. He liked the company of women, but he didn't need it. Mostly he looked to them for entertainment. For conversation, not for kicks. The physical side of things, if it happened at all, was a bonus. Even then, women rarely delivered all they promised. Boys were somehow wired differently. Pleasure never had to be negotiated.

Plus, he dreaded women of the type his mother wanted him to date. Dependable, long-legged girls, who wanted to choose his shirts, cook his meals, and raise his children: homebuilders. Yet they pursued him. Worse still, they were highly adept at disguise. Strip away the lipstick and lingerie from most women and you'd find a homebuilder in waiting.

That's why he was so fascinated by Candy and now Nola: his own *Deux Anglaises*. They were unlike any women he'd met before. There was a spirit of independence, as if they didn't give a damn about the world, or how it judged them. Nola especially: 'If you think about it', she said, 'all women are rewarded for sex, one way or another. Some get diamonds or furs, or holidays abroad. I ask for cash — that's the only difference. It's up to me how I spend it.'

Yet though Candy and Nola stood apart from the rest, they were quite different from one another. Nola was clever, confident, exciting. Did he want to sleep with her? Yes, of course, for the hell of it. But not if it meant losing the thrill of their assignations.

Candy was more complex. She was intelligent and considerate, but not playful like Nola; not 'smart'. He was fond of her; he missed her; but he didn't feel the urge to be with her, to touch her, to taste her. Nola had got under his skin.

13

Alone at home, Candy was a secret sybarite. Mornings began with a leisurely bath, perfumed with a dash of coconut milk soak. Breakfast was another private ritual: freshly ground coffee and orange juice, with a croissant or brioche, still warm from the bakery.

This morning was unusual, though. Something was missing from her routine. Her period was three days late, and normally she was as regular as clockwork. It didn't need a genius to work out why. The only mystery was why it had taken her so long to get him into bed. But until recently Luke had been hooked up with Alice, so strictly off limits.

Alice must have known how much she fancied him, because she always delighted in telling her, in precise and unnecessary detail, how wonderfully compliant he was in the sack. For some people, talking about sex seemed to be as natural a part of the post-coital experience as smoking was for others. It was the commitment thing that had forced them apart. Luke wanted kids, Alice didn't; he wanted her to stop playing the field, she refused. The usual stuff.

Now that he was footloose, he was more handsome than ever. And everything that Alice had said was true — in spades. So keen to please, so willing to be abused. So typical of him to hit the target at the first attempt.

The phone rang as she stubbed out her cigarette, the first of two she currently allowed herself each day, although today could prove an exception.

'George? What on earth are you doing up so early?'

'I have some news ... I had a drink with an old friend on the force a couple of weeks ago. He promised to let me know if Margrét appeared on their radar. He's just called. Said they've got a girl in the morgue at Paddington and wondered if we might be able to ID her.'

'Oh', she said. 'What makes you think it's Margrét?'

'She has red stars tattooed on her back.'

'Where did they find her?'

'Down by the canal.'

'Do they know how she died?'

'No, but they did say she'd been cut quite a bit.'

Candy shuddered. 'Let me think about it', she said. 'I'm still waking up. Call me back in half an hour.'

* * *

The morgue was subterranean and windowless. An air-conditioning unit buzzed irritably, fluorescent lights flickered; the smell of death and disinfectant had got into the walls.

'This is the girl', said the young police officer. 'They brought her in two nights ago.'

Candy glanced at the pale face and turned away. 'It's not Margrét.'

'Are you sure ma'am?' asked the officer: 'She does fit the general description.'

'Absolutely certain. I'd know her anywhere, even in this state. It's not her.'

'I'm sorry ... but the star tattoo corresponds, surely?'

'It's a common enough motif', she replied. Margrét's stars ran the length of her spine, but she saw no point in mentioning it.

'Back to square one then', said George. The policewoman closed her notebook, obviously disappointed.

'Have you established cause of death yet?' George asked.

'We're waiting for toxicology reports. We won't know for sure until next week.'

'Oh, I see ... Well, I'm sorry we couldn't help.'

'Thank you for coming', said the officer: 'We'll have to make further enquiries.'

The silent attendant zipped up the bag. The girl on the gurney still had no name. Candy gripped George's wrist. 'Take me home', she said quietly.

George dropped her at the end of the mews, and she walked the last few yards to her front door, feeling cold and vulnerable. It wasn't the fact of the girl's death that disturbed her. It was being confronted with it in such a perfunctory manner. The kid couldn't have been more than eighteen, maybe even younger. Pretty in a damaged kind of way, but far too thin. And no marks for guessing she was a user. Another broken doll working the streets. Except no longer, poor little tyke.

How would she have reacted had it been Margrét? No different probably. She barely knew her. Even though they'd spent so much time together, there was no emotional connection, no bond. She didn't even hate her. But she'd get there, given time.

After the morgue she felt dirty: contaminated. She lit a scented candle and ran another bath. While she waited for the tub to fill, she set the little Bialetti espresso maker on the hob, then on impulse dialled Luke's number at the hospital. She was surprised to get straight through.

'What's the emergency this time?' he asked; 'I hope you haven't got yourself into another fight?'

'No, nothing's wrong. Nothing like that anyway.' The coffee pot hissed and gurgled, and she took it off the gas. 'It's just that if you were free, I'd love it if you could come over this evening. I'll cook something.'

'Now that sounds too good to be true. What's the catch?'

'You'll see …'

* * *

Having consulted Elizabeth David, Candy drove to Holland Park. At Lidgate's she bought veal escalopes, cut from the filet mignon. Escalopes Savoyardes: nothing but the best for the doctor. At the pharmacy she picked up a pregnancy testing kit. Better be sure, before turning a drama into a crisis. The pharmacist eyed her suspiciously, as if asking why she'd been so stupid as to get herself knocked up. Good question. But it was so long since she'd been with anyone that the Pill had never seemed necessary.

On the way home, she stopped off at her rooms to accessorise. The house was quiet, and nothing appeared to have changed since her last visit, other than the deepening layer of dust. Opening the shutters revealed a billion microscopic motes somersaulting in the sunlight: particles of human hair and skin, bits of birds' feathers and butterflies' wings, desiccated shit, and chimney soot. Everyone knows what it is, but how it accumulates, even in a sealed room, is one of life's enduring mysteries.

Left to her own devices, Candy never dusted. In any case she had no need to. Margrét cleaned and polished, as every maid should. And at home she had Mrs Hall, who looked after her once a week. Dear old Mrs Hall. Now there was a cautionary tale: the moral decline of a working girl from Bethnal Green. From hotel chambermaid to hooker; thirty years on the game and now a charlady. Once a scrubber always a scrubber.

Only as she turned towards the dressing room did it occur to her that she'd left the shutters open when she left last time. Somebody had closed them: but who? Olga, possibly, though if she wanted to use the room she usually called. Or one of the dillies upstairs, venturing off piste. Whoever it was, it had to be someone with a key. Burglars, as a rule, don't lock up.

The silence on the stairs told her that Olga was away, or out, so the answer would have to wait. Intrigued, she began to look for other signs of intrusion: a stray hair on the sofa, perhaps; or a spent lipstick on the dressing table. It amused her for a while, poking about, searching for clues, playing Maigret instead of fretting about Margrét, but nothing leapt out.

Tiring of the charade, she returned to the dressing room and the task at hand. From the bottom of the wardrobe, she took a leather holdall, unzipping it to check its contents. Then from beneath the day bed she pulled out a long canvas bag. It rattled and she pushed it back — wrong one. The second bag was overstuffed and far heavier than its size suggested; it was what she wanted. That was everything.

She locked the wardrobe then slung the holdall over her shoulder and dragged the kit bag into the salon, leaving a broad impression in the carpet. Standing in the doorway she gave the room a final glance.

Generally, the carpet's paisley pattern had a camouflaging effect: 'So practical dear, it won't show the stains', as Olga had observed. But where the heavy bag had flattened the pile, the light caught it differently and she saw something. There amid the swirl of greens and golds was a sprinkling of brown spots.

She dropped the bags and knelt to investigate. Scratching at the clotted fibres released a little crop of powder, which she dabbed with a wet finger. The metallic taste was unmistakable: blood. Two scenarios flashed up immediately: murder or menstruation. If that messy little cunt Margrét had bled on the carpet she'd kill her anyway.

14

Candy untied the kit bag and pulled out the heavy roll. It looked like a furled rubber tent with tubular plastic poles. Then she set to work assembling it, spreading the sheeting over her mattress, clipping the lengths of tubing together and sliding them inside their sleeves to form a frame around the edge of the bed. The final arrangement was secured at the corners with long rubber straps. From the holdall, she took a vacuum pump with a flexible hose, which plugged into a grommet in the top sheet. She flicked the switch. Good — it worked.

The vacbed provides the most exquisite form of restraint. You lie cocooned in latex. As the air around you is pumped out, the material is drawn closer to your body until movement is impossible. You cannot see, touch, smell, or taste. Deprived of four senses, the fifth is heightened. Sounds that would not normally register are amplified. You hear your heart pounding and the blood coursing through your veins. To be held captive in this way is to experience a feeling of otherworldliness, like floating on a heavenly sea. Oh, and one more detail. Sexual satisfaction, if attained, is raised to new levels of intensity. This bed had been custom-made to allow just that.

The doorbell rang shortly after seven. 'I came straight from the ward', Luke said, slipping off his overcoat. 'I didn't want to be late … I knew I'd be in trouble if I kept you waiting.' He was early. A little too keen, possibly.

'You're in trouble already.' She said, taking hold of his tie and pulling him close. 'One question before I take you upstairs: you're not claustrophobic, are you?'

'No, I don't think so.'

'Good, because this is going to take a while …'

Immobile in his transparent rubber sac, Luke lay spread out on the bed like a shrink-wrapped ready meal. A boil-in-the-bag boyfriend. Candy admired her new plaything, walking slowly around the foot of the bed, assessing him from different angles … a perfect arrangement.

76

She undressed slowly, leaving her clothes where they fell, then armed with a bottle of lube, mounted him, and smoothed the liquid across the latex and over her skin until both bodies glistened. He was deliciously warm and slippery beneath her, better even than in the flesh.

She began slowly, keeping time with the metronomic *put put put* of the pump. When she sensed he might be about to come, she eased herself off and began again in a new torture spot. Suddenly he began to buck violently. Fuck! She'd kinked his breathing tube. Careful, don't want to suffocate the poor lamb. Not yet anyway.

* * *

Candy seasoned the veal and dropped the pieces into the hot butter; they sizzled, and she flipped them over. Then she added a slug of vermouth, straight from the bottle. It frothed in the pan. After tormenting him, it was a peculiar pleasure to cook for him, to act the part of the dutiful girlfriend, a new role with everything to learn.

'This is the perfect dish for a sadistic chef', said Luke. 'Cut from an animal reared in cruelty.'

'I hoped you'd approve …' She turned down the heat and stirred a carton of cream into the bubbling liquid. 'And I made sure the cream was whipped.'

Luke laughed: 'I would expect nothing less.'

'This needs to simmer for a couple of minutes and then we can eat. Would you mind taking the spuds to the table? Thanks. And there's a salad.'

'This veal is so tender', said Luke. 'You have so many talents, I don't know which to compliment you on first.'

'Here, have some more wine', said Candy, refilling his glass. She paused for a moment, unsure how to continue the conversation. 'Have you ever seen a corpse?'

'One or two …'

'Sorry, silly question.'

'Why do you ask?'

'George took me to the morgue this morning. They had a girl in there. The police thought it could be Margrét. They wanted me to identify her.'

Luke looked at her quizzically, as if only half believing: 'And was it her?'

'No, it was some little tyke I've never seen before. A druggie, by the look of her. No more than a kid. They said she'd been cut up. Fortunately, I didn't have to look.'

'Cut up like you were, you mean?'

'Not exactly ... "deep incisions to the mons pubis" is what George said.'

'Sounds like variations on a familiar theme to me. What else did George say? I can tell that's not the whole story.'

'No really, that's it. I haven't told him what happened to me. Only that I want to find Margrét and Diessel. He keeps probing though. He's not stupid; he knows something's up.'

'Perhaps you should confide in him. He may be able to help. You should have gone to the police right at the beginning.'

'I know, but I don't trust the fuzz. Nor does Olga. And I don't see Diessel as a killer, somehow. Just a pervert. People like that always want fresh blood and he's had his fun with me. But then I keep seeing that poor little kid on the slab ...' She began to cry, silently and spontaneously. Big dollopy tears landed on the table. Shit! That wasn't in the script. Reaching across, she cupped Luke's hands in hers. 'Will you stay? I really don't want to be alone tonight ... there's something else I've got to tell you.'

15

Nola hadn't returned Oliver's calls. A week had passed, in which his mood had darkened, his appetite had vanished, and his smoking had reached the upper twenties. But he was on the way up again. Despondency had yielded to indignation, and he had begun not to care.

He heard the phone as he reached the top of the stairs, but before he could get his key in the lock the machine clicked in. He recognised her voice on the other side of the door: '*Ollie — hi, it's me. I've been away — call me.*' He called her straight back, but her line was engaged, so he left a message in turn. Later that afternoon she rang again.

'I missed you ... where have you been?' he asked.

'You mean all your life or for the past week?'

'The last few days will do.'

'In Rio', she said. 'Copacabana. Sunning myself on the beach.'

'I envy you ... who was the lucky man?' He tried to sound offhand but failed.

'There was no man. I went by myself. It's an annual ritual. I like to have time alone occasionally. Not tonight, though. I'm free if you'd like to have dinner.'

His mood somersaulted in an instant.

* * *

The Café Royal could have been a set for *Dynasty*: a gilded performance space for black-suited Mayfair men of a certain age and their white-stilettoed escorts. Oliver and Nola had a table near the entrance, not the best in the house, but a perfect vantage point from which to observe the players coming and going. 'I'm waiting for Blake and Krystle to drop in next', he said, eyeing a particularly effete couple.

'I'm more of an Alexis girl myself', said Nola, scanning the restaurant. 'You know, this place has hookers like dogs have fleas. I guarantee there are at least half a dozen here already — present company excepted.'

'How can you tell?'

'It's not so difficult. You can always spot them. Start with her clothes and make-up. She'll be immaculate. She'll wear stockings, never tights. Most women let standards slip somewhere along the line — their nails or their leg wax, say — but not the professional girl. She can't afford to.'

'I hadn't thought about that.'

'Okay', she said, 'at three o'clock from you ... dark hair, wearing an Armani bolero jacket and jade earrings.'

Two tables away, a girl in her twenties was with a much older man; they had little conversation.

'I see her, but how do you know so much about the jacket?'

'It's this season's ... I saw it in Harvey Nicks this afternoon.'

'And what makes you think she's a pro?'

'Can't you see her shoes?'

'Just about. What's so special about them?'

'You can judge a woman's interest in you by the height of her heels. They're not called "fuck-me shoes" for nothing. If she wears flats on a date you know you're heading for the rocks. Hers are right up there, so she's either super excited, or she wants him to think she is. What's your guess?'

'It's hard to believe anyone that young would be interested in grandpa over there.'

'Precisely. Now look at her ankles.'

'They're nice ... very slim.'

'No, I mean what she's wearing. Her stockings are silk. You can tell that by the way they ruckle slightly. Silk doesn't stretch like nylon. It's a sure sign. Now see how she drinks.'

He studied her for a minute, trying to look as if he were lost in contemplation, instead of gaping like an idiot.

'She's hardly drinking at all.'

'Now look at the guy ... he's knocking it back.'

'She's cool, he's nervous.'

'Exactly. He may be the one with the money, but she's the one in control.'

He brushed his lighter onto the floor casually and checked Nola's heels as he reached down to pick it up. Medium to high, nothing to be concerned about.

Over coffee, he summoned his courage: 'I'd really like to take you home. It's not much of a place, but at least it's mine. And it's not too far. We can be there in ten minutes in a cab.'

She looked at him severely and folded her napkin. 'Don't worry, it's all taken care of. I've got a room at Brown's; we can go straight up. And before you ask, yes, I have a spare toothbrush.'

* * *

Nola unlocked the door and ushered Oliver in. The room was large and comfortable in an old-fashioned way. It could have been his grandparents' house in Sussex, except that it was uncomfortably warm, not bone-numbingly cold. An enormous bed looked as if it could sleep three, and quite possibly had.

'So, this is how the other half lives', he said.

Nola threw her fur onto a chair. 'I won't be a minute, I'm going to change', she said, heading to the bathroom. 'Why don't you fix us both a drink.' Even the minibar was a minor work of art, carefully concealed within a Chinoiserie cabinet.

'Okay, you can come in now!' she called. He opened the door halfway and peered in. She was perched on the edge of the bath, naked, watching the water gush in from a wide nickel spout. 'Come … I won't bite!'

Her neck and body were sprinkled with moles, delicate little marks not much more than freckles: tiny imperfections that made her beauty seem all the more complete. They kissed and he caught the ghosts of warm Armagnac and dark chocolate. She linked her arms around his waist and squeezed. 'Thank you for dinner', she said. 'It was lovely.'

'It was my pleasure.'

'I've brought a little something to get us in the mood', she said, indicating two lines on the counter. She handed him a rolled twenty: 'After you …'

'Ah, I'm afraid I'm not entirely sure of the etiquette', he replied, realising he'd awarded himself a black mark.

'Oh, I see … you surprise me. Well, it's simple. You hold the note like this … then you take it up like this.' Nola snorted a line then dabbed her septum. 'There, it's easy. But as it's your first time, you'd better start with a bit less.' She cut a new line with her

Diners' card and passed him the note. 'Here ...'

Fffmmhh! A nasal burn, then a spreading numbness in the throat. The aftertaste was bitter, almost medicinal, strange but not unpleasant. Was that it? Then gradually he grew sharper, stronger, more focused, more aroused, ready to conquer anything and everything. Euphoric: a master of the universe. Nola ran her hand over his crotch and squeezed: 'Come big boy, we've got enough Charlie to keep us going all night.'

He paid the bill on the way out. She hadn't mentioned it but somehow, he knew it was expected. Perhaps that was another test. Whatever it cost, it had been worth it. Being with her had been so exhilarating, so perfect, that when he awoke, he'd had the urge to scoop her up and do it all over again, but she'd politely sent him on his way. Would it happen again? She hadn't said as much. But then she'd kissed him affectionately when he left, so perhaps he shouldn't worry.

How much would he tell Jan? Nothing, if he had any sense; but everything, probably, once the alcohol began to talk: 'You'll never guess what happened to me? I slept with a nightclub hostess. *A real pro!*' He pictured Jan's jaw dropping. 'Yes, and do you know what? It was the most amazing night of my life.' He strode along with giant's steps, suddenly seven feet tall.

16

Tower Bridge stood out brightly in the morning sunlight, its stone piers seeming to rest on the blanket of mist that clung to the incoming tide. He rarely ventured south of the river if he could avoid it. He associated it with a particularly fruitless period in his life. It was another city. Indeed, for the most part it was barely a city at all, merely the brittle edge of the suburbs. Living there sapped the soul.

Beyond the bridge, a melancholy scene of urban abandonment unfolded. He turned off the main road and parked the car.

A dark canyon of warehouses ran along the river's edge. Greenery abounded in the gutters and sprouted from the brickwork. Iron walkways laced between sheer masonry walls. One of the buildings had lost its doors and he ventured in, imagining cinnamon, caraway, ginger, and cumin, all vanished long ago.

He reached the end of the street without seeing anyone, then threaded his way back through the empty alleyways. As he neared the bridge again, he found signs of habitation. A few pioneers had set up studios in one of the warehouses and he found Alice Man's name among them.

A bare bulb shone dimly in the hallway and there was hardly more light on the stairs. The stone treads had been sculpted and smoothed through a century of use, each step having to be judged on its merits.

After three flights he found a grey metal door with a small black card attached to it. He knocked, but there was no reply. Then the door gave slightly, and he saw that it was off the latch. He pushed it open and went in. A naked blonde was strapped to a padded wooden frame, bent double so that her buttocks formed the apex of a fleshy, invitational triangle.

'Oh, excuse me … I'm so sorry.'

The girl looked at him but did not respond.

'Who's there?' said a voice. 'Just a second … I'm in the darkroom.'

'Alice?' he called. 'Is that you? It's me, Oliver!'

He barely recognised her when she emerged. Her hair was bound up in a red cotton scarf, and she wore a thick blue sweater over denim dungarees. She could have been a stand-in for Rosie the Riveter, the pin-up for the American war effort. 'Hi', she said. 'What a nice surprise.'

'I thought I'd try my luck. I hope I'm not interrupting anything?'

'No, not at all. I've been printing for a couple hours. I need to take a break. My exhibition opens next week … at the Lens Gallery in Charlotte Street. You must come.'

'I'd love to, thanks.'

He glanced at the blonde. 'This is Christiane', said Alice, smacking the girl sharply on the bottom. 'She doesn't speak much English, but she's very accommodating. She'll be happy like that for a while.'

The loft spread out forever; but the ceiling was low, and the bare brick walls absorbed what little daylight penetrated the grime on the windows. A tangle of cables connected a miscellany of studio lights. If Alice had switched them on the place might have been warmer.

Gradually he took in the secondary details of the room. Next to an old leather sofa, a dog was curled up in a basket, its grey snout poking from beneath a woollen blanket. 'He's called Severin', Alice said, following his gaze. 'He's been with me since he was a puppy. He's completely devoted to his mistress.'

Severin ... Severin? *Venus in Furs*, of course. Severin, the archetypal willing slave. An obvious connection, perhaps. But the moral of that story is ambiguous. The slave ends up despising the mistress, and the mistress ultimately tires of the slave. Severin, the fettered masochist, emerges as a sadist, and his mistress turns submissive. Relationships are never as straightforward as they seem. Alice most likely assumed the dominant role. Just look at that poor girl on the frame. But what was the dynamic between Alice and Candy?

Framed photographs were propped against the walls. Curious, confident faces stared back at him. There was a striking black-and-white shot of Liza standing in the lobby at Maitresse, wearing the rubber sheath dress she'd worn the night they met. She held a cigarette nonchalantly and the palm of her free hand was planted flat against the wall, as if for support.

In a different sequence of images, female figures were meticulously bound with rope. 'It's an ancient technique, called *Kinbaku*', Alice explained. 'I learned it from a Japanese rope master. I find it meditative; and being bound is divine.'

She pulled out another frame and turned it to the light: 'I took this one of Candy a couple of months ago.' It was a nude study, shot from behind. Candy's back was covered with an elaborate tattoo — a trippy exercise in the style of Roger Dean. A dozen or more butterflies hovered above a full-blown amber rose, whose faded petals looked ready to drop.

'This is her too, but I guess you might recognise her this time.' Candy wore a tight rubber vest with inflatable breasts, like pneumatic missiles. But it was her face that interested him most: the eyes again, just like the Mapplethorpe picture. Her gaze was direct and defiant. Quite different from the quiet, contemplative Candy he knew. 'I call this one *Eldorado*', Alice said.

'After the Cadillac Eldorado?'

'Yeah, my dad had a '59 convertible when I was a kid in Pasadena. It wallowed like a boat, but I loved that bullet detail on the tailfins.' She picked the photograph up and handed it to him. 'The *Guardian* said this piece was "school of Helmut Newton" but I'm not sure. What do you think?'

'It's not a connection I would have made', he said.

'Explain ...'

'Well, I would say that Newton likes to draw you into the position of voyeur, as if you're complicit in his world. With your women I get the sense that they're looking at me. Your photographs are about sexuality, but they're not meant to be *sexy*.' She smiled, obviously pleased. 'And Newton's women are posed and unattainable. To me they feel cold. But your women are very much alive. They seem self-possessed, vital.' Some of them were also more than a little frightening.

'I despise Newton and everything he represents,' she said, almost spitting out the name. 'My photographs are not *erotic*. My people have real lives and real passions. What I'm trying to do is to get them to reveal something about themselves. For me, the image is part of a much bigger picture. A life story.'

'As if the shutter were merely the blinking of an eye.'

'Exactly!' she said. 'I'm glad you understand. I think we'll get along fine.'

As he was leaving, he said as casually as he could: 'I should have asked you before: how do I find Candy? I don't even know her last name, or where she lives.'

'You know, honestly, I have no idea', she said, and he was inclined to believe her. 'She's always been plain Candy. I see her at Maitresse, or she comes here. We've never had need of formalities.'

'But you must have a phone number?'

'I can give you her business number if you want. It's all I have.'

'Her *business* number ... what sort of business?'

'Candy's a pro-domme. Mistress Candide. Didn't she tell you?'

'No, she told me she was a tart.'

'She did? Well, she has many strings to her bow, but I can imagine her saying that, to get a rise out of you. Let's just say she has an extensive professional interest in sex. She's one of the best.'

He rang the number when he got home and wasn't surprised to hear a recorded message. He was going to hang up but changed his mind.

'Candy ... Hello it's Oliver. I hope this is the right number. I've missed your visits. You can call me at home, any time. I'd really love to see you.' He wanted to say more, but left his number then hung up.

17

Alice was waiting at the Lens Gallery. 'Good to see you again, Oliver!' she said, 'Welcome to my world.' The familiar fringe was restored, above black-lined eyes; her face was pale and mask-like, her mouth a vivid red. She stood like an acrobat, her body taut, poised ready to spring.

The gallery wasn't busy. The greyhound Severin lay quietly in one corner, head on paws, eyes half open, watchful. A Punk couple, with matching Mohicans, were studying the pictures as if looking for familiar faces; and Alice's dealer was there, talking to a tall, dark-suited gentleman with a closely cropped skull. A client, he assumed.

Alice led him to a photograph of a woman with two lines of metal D-rings let into her back. Scarlet braid was wound through the rings, and she had a line of tiny red stars tattooed down her spine. It brought to mind a Horst P Horst image, *Mainbocher Corset*. 'This is Margrét', said Alice. 'She's relatively new on the scene, but I think she has great promise. I was pleased when she got that done. I plan to do more with her.'

'Doesn't it hurt?' he said.

'The procedure? Sure, but that's part of the attraction. Some people thrive on pain. It's a way of testing limits; it changes the way you relate to your body. Here, let me show you something ...'

She guided him to another work, a detail of a female figure, whose pale skin had been transformed into a battlescape of raised and puckered scar tissue. The effect was strangely compelling, like a mutilated *Venus*, attractive in a way that transcended conventional notions of beauty.

'This is Christiane ... you saw her in the studio, remember? I found her in a club in Hamburg and brought her over. She's *very* special. Look, isn't it amazing? It's kinda like a land art piece in miniature.'

The gallerist interrupted. 'Alice, this is Mister Pedersen, he's just purchased *Lacing*.'

Pedersen bowed his head. 'Delighted to meet you Miss Man.'

Alice looked at him appraisingly. 'Are you a collector Mister Pedersen?'

'In a small way', he said.

'And what do you collect, apart from photographs?'

'I like to acquire exquisite things of all kinds. The more fragile, the better.'

'Aren't you afraid they will break?'

'No, but I sometimes like to take them to the point of breaking.'

'Then I believe we may have something in common.'

The vibration between them was palpable, but clearly didn't extend to Oliver. So, he left them to their love-in and focused his attention on the photographs. Most he remembered from Alice's studio, but there was a new series in sepia tone, which he hadn't seen before. They were quite different from her other work, pure explorations of the female form, with naked figures superimposed in multiple exposures.

'Tell me about these', he said, when Alice returned. 'I think they're very special.'

'Thank you! I was printing them when you stopped by the other day. They're an experiment really.'

There were several women in the pictures — sometimes three or four juxtaposed. But one slender body provided a leitmotiv. She had small, firm breasts, like a figure from a Tamara de Lempicka painting. Her skin was pale, almost translucent, the filigree of her veins visible beneath the surface. She was usually placed behind the others, as if reluctant to be seen. He sensed that the series was somehow confessional. 'Have you ever made a self-portrait?' he asked.

'Clever boy', she said. 'I wondered how long you'd take to work it out.'

Alice suggested lunch, and they opted for L'Etoile, which was right across the street. It was old school and one of his favourite haunts. La Patronne, Elena, had lined the restaurant with photographs of legendary diners, most as old and yellow as the walls. He was pointing out Francis Bacon when the man himself brushed past, flashing a Rolex the size of the moon.

'What an extraordinary face he has', said Alice, once he was out of earshot. 'It's like seeing him through a fisheye lens.'

'He comes here all the time. Usually with a pretty rough crowd. Perhaps you should photograph him. I could introduce you if you'd like.'

'No need', she said, 'Those *rough* friends of his are regulars at the club.'

So, Alice's social connections were more extensive than he'd imagined. And her emphasis on *rough* said be careful. But other than the fact that she'd grown up on the West Coast, she hadn't given much away. He knew not to ask too many questions, though.

People often reveal more about themselves if you give them an opening and let them talk.

'You were playing Sade's *When Am I Going to Make a Living* in the gallery', he said. 'I thought that was very witty.'

'Yeah, I love her. I chose that track to wind my dealer up. He's always trying to jip me.'

'I like her too. She has such an original look.'

'She's part British, part Nigerian. Cocktails are always more interesting than straight up, don't you think?'

'I agree. But people here are usually suspicious of anything exotic.'

'You get that everywhere. When I was in high school, kids would make the slitty eye thing. There was a lot of anti-Jap prejudice in the States back then.'

'But you're not Japanese?'

'Well, I suppose I am in a way. On my mother's side.'

She took a long drag on her cigarette; maybe that was all he was getting. But then she began again.

'My grandma was a comfort girl, what the Japanese called *jugun ianfu*. The Japanese prized Korean girls above all others, and she was particularly beautiful. She was fourteen when they took her ... just a kid. She was playing in the street one day, when a car drew up. It was a small village, so they probably hadn't seen many cars. The driver asked her if she'd like a ride and, knowing no better, she got in. That was the last she saw of her family.'

'Where did they take her?'

'To a camp somewhere. What they called a comfort station. In a way she was fortunate. The commandant kept her for himself. Eventually she fell pregnant, but he allowed her to keep the child; even brought her up in his own way. The child was my mom.'

She paused again, and he ordered another glass of wine from the waiter, who was hovering, ears flapping.

'When the Americans finally came, the guards killed most of the girls. But the commandant shut my grandma and my mom in a cellar and left them there. He must have known they might starve, but at least he gave them a chance.'

'What happened next?'

'I don't know exactly. They were taken to a nursing home. And at some point, my gran met my grandpa, or my step-grandpa. He was an Army doctor. He took them back to the States at the end of the war.'

'Are your parents still alive?'

'My dad yes, he's a big strong American boy. Farming stock. My mom no. She died last year. Got cancer and faded away. She told me she was very happy for most of her life. Said she always regarded herself as lucky, though in a way I think she felt guilty for having survived.'

He asked her about growing up in LA, imagining a sun-kissed slice of the American dream. Instead, she told him about teenage sex parties in West Hollywood, and her first steps in the underground scene.

'I had a lotta fun. I got laid. I did other stuff I probably shouldn't have. But I was never really at home in California. You know the real problem with LA is that too many people regard sex as basically part of their workout programme. For them it's all about calories and muscle tone. They don't understand that the brain is the primary sexual organ. People here at least get that.'

'Is that why you moved East?'

'Partly that. When I was eighteen, I hooked up with a Dutch guy who used to photograph the acts at CBGB and Max's Kansas City. I followed him to New York.'

'What were the clubs like there?'

'Way more interesting. There was a place in SoHo called The Loft where we'd sometimes spend the night. Iggy Pop used to drop in. Patti Smith too. And you could do pretty much as you pleased. Deal was you took your own booze, kinda like dropping in on a private party.'

'SoHo must have seemed like the centre of the Universe back then.'

'It was — SoHo and the East Village.'

'Where else did you go?'

'A whole lot of dives, some of them pretty wild. There were places in the Meatpacking District you could find anything your kinky little heart desired. Still can if you want.'

'What were they like?'

'Listen, I don't think this is a conversation for a public place. Let's just say they were way edgier than Maitresse. You should ask Candy next time you see her. She's the expert.'

'You're talking about the Hellfire, right?'

'Okay, so you know about that place. Interesting, I would never have guessed.'

'Only by reputation. Is it still there?' Should he mention the Mapplethorpe picture? No, let her bring it up.

'Very much so, and just as badass as it ever was. I should go visit, to remind myself what the scene's capable of. You know, the club here plays it so safe. They're terrified they'll get raided. People are dressed up like they should be getting it on, but instead they're talking about vacations or school fees or crap like that. It's way too middle class for me, but it's the best we've got.'

'I got that feeling too, but then it's all new to me.'

'On the whole I find the fetish scene more satisfying as still life than real life,' she said.

'Do you think people are less inhibited in New York, is that it?'

'For sure. I was invited along to Studio 54 once, just before I left New York actually. That place was something else. Up on the balconies people really got it going. I saw Frank Sinatra getting blown by a Chinese girl. I was going to say, beautiful Chinese girl, but I never got to see her face. His was a picture though.'

'I can imagine.'

The waiter brought coffee; time was running out, so he went for broke: 'Tell me how you and Candy first met.'

'I guessed you'd ask about that', she said. 'It was at the Windmill. I went backstage to photograph the girls for a feature in one of the colour supplements. You know the kind of thing: "Secret London: the city that never sleeps". She stood out as being special and I took to her. Back then she was living in a squat behind Fitzroy Square. Boy George and Marilyn and a bunch of other freewheeling people lived round the corner. We used to hang out together at Blitz. And then you *really* had to dress up, otherwise Steve wouldn't let you in. It was always full of fabulous creatures.'

'Steve?'

'Steve Strange. He could be a real bitch if he didn't like the look of you. I was there one night when Mick Jagger pitched up and Steve said take a hike. The thing was he got there too late. You literally couldn't have got anyone else in. We all thought it was hilarious, of course, but Jagger was mad as fuck.'

'Did you photograph Candy then too?'

'Yeah, on and off. I did some stuff for *i-D*. Then Nick Logan asked me to shoot a cover for *The Face* and I chose Candy. She had a flat top back then, so I put her in white tie and gave her a Dietrich vibe. She could've made it big as a model. She's way more photogenic than Jerry Hall, in my humble opinion. Better legs too. But she hated the attention. She's more twilight than limelight.'

'But you've shot her a lot since. She must enjoy it, or am I wrong?'

'She's a very private person. What I do now is different from magazine work. You're not gonna wake up one morning and find your face on a billboard or plastered on the side of the bus. That's what freaked her out. Now, she's totally cool about it. I rely on her a lot.'

'You mean in the sense that she's your muse?'

'Kinda like that. The way I work with Candy is completely unselfconscious, on both sides.'

'Of all your portraits, I think that those of Candy are the most intimate. You can see that she looks at you differently from the others. She seems to be throwing down a challenge.'

'You're right. But perhaps that's because she has a better sense of self than most people. I think the camera captures that.'

He paid the bill and got up, ready to go. But Alice remained seated, looking at him, almost into him. 'I've told you more than I intended', she said finally. 'Now I have a question for you. You don't have to respond right now. But I want you to think about it and when you're ready, maybe come and talk.'

He sat down again, uncertain how long she would take, or how to respond.

'I can see from your aura, Oliver, that you're a deeply conflict-ed individual. I may be able to help direct you, but first I need you to look inside yourself, peel away your defences, trust your intuition.' Another pause. 'I want to know what excites you. What *really* turns you on?'

Her eyes drilled as she waited for an answer. But what was he supposed to say? None of your business, actually.

'Okay, let's try looking at it from the opposite direction', she said. 'Sometimes it helps to articulate what you fear most', she of-fered. 'What might that be?'

That thorny little question could be answered in just two words: Henry Pound. Henry had managed to live his entire life as a lie. In fact, it was his only real achievement. Even his funeral had been a travesty. They'd held the service in St Margaret's, Westminster, the church where Henry and Holly had been married. All the cab-inet had been there, larger than life, apart from Norman Tebbit, of course; he'd probably be in the sick bay for months, poor old bugger. Mrs T had looked otherworldly, as if she'd been recast as Saint Joan. She'd even spoken of Henry confidentially as 'another Tory martyr'. Norman St John-Stevas had struggled through his oration, clearly grief-stricken. And Holly appeared to have shrunk several sizes, as if the humiliation were too much to bear. All be-cause Henry had been incapable of honesty.

'I suppose the prospect of dying before I've found what I'm looking for. Of being cheated somehow. Or having to settle for compromise.'

'But you're young. I don't understand.'

'I know, but I'm afraid that what I'm looking for may be unat-tainable. That it's like some unverifiable hypothesis. Sometimes I feel as if I'm trying to find something I know must be out there. If not right here, then somewhere in the world. But it always seems beyond my reach.'

'You should try not to over-intellectualise, Oliver. In my ex-perience you can find pretty much anything, once you know what you're looking for. Is that the only thing you're afraid of?'

'I'm wary of intimacy, I suppose.'

'Are you saying you don't like sex?'

'No, I mean what comes before and after sex. The enforced closeness, the lack of freedom. The constant need for affection.'

'That sounds more like a fear of commitment.'

'Possibly. I've always imagined myself being alone. But now I'm beginning to think I might want the best of both worlds — the security of a relationship, but with none of the emotional baggage.'

'It's a game for you, isn't it?'

'Does that matter?'

'It depends how badly you mind losing.' He caught the sharp note of irritation in her voice. 'You know, I can't help you unless you really want to be guided.'

'I'm sorry. It's just that I find it difficult to put what I want into words.'

'That could explain why you haven't been successful.' She paused. 'Okay. Let's try to make it a little easier. Imagine yourself alone at night, in bed. You're tired, maybe a little drunk, completely relaxed. In that special moment, before you slide into sleep, you fantasise. What is it that you imagine doing? What secret place do you visit?'

It was a place he returned to frequently: the setting and the act were always the same. But how could she possibly know? And what right did she have to be so inquisitorial? Americans were so gauche. In any case, it wasn't that simple. Even if he were to find the thing he craved, sometimes he doubted whether he'd be strong enough to embrace it. After Henry's sorry dénouement, the likelihood of dying unfulfilled nagged more than ever.

* * *

Farewell to Henry Pound the brave, who lived ten weeks from groom to grave. Thanks to *The Sun* for that jaunty little epitaph. Eleven-and-a-bit weeks, in fact, but then that didn't fit nearly so well. Oliver tossed the newspaper away in disgust. The pages skittered across the floor, coming to rest in a heap at the base of the bookshelves.

And then it dawned. Candy had left a clue and it had been right under his nose all along. The day after he'd found her on his doorstep, she'd pushed a pencilled note through his letterbox. For some reason he'd kept it, tucked in next to Camus under 'C' on his shelves. Her handwriting was small and almost forensically precise, the upper strokes long and upright. She'd written on the back of an envelope, which had been torn in half. It bore a fragment of an address: the last four letters of a name — *dens* — and then *Mews*. He found the *London A—Z* and scanned the index. To his surprise, he discovered that there were relatively few mews in the city. Maybe it wouldn't be so difficult after all?

Within an hour he had it — Hyde Park Gardens Mews. It was a little passage that ran parallel with the park. He knew it. Lucie Rie had her studio there, and it was only ten minutes' walk away.

A spattering of raindrops pockmarked the ground, and the sky had that steel-grey luminosity which precedes a heavy fall. The street was quiet, as if in anticipation. He set off anyway, walking briskly, on a mission. As he got to Lancaster Gate, it began to rain in earnest. By the time he reached the mews he was soaked.

It was a perfect backwater. Other than a lick of paint, it couldn't have changed much in a century. Although now it was classic pied-à-terre territory, and the garages would house BMWs not broughams. It didn't tally with the image he'd developed of Candy and her lifestyle; he was obviously missing something.

Though the light was fading, few of the windows were lit up, a sure sign that people had left for the weekend. Even Lucie's studio was dark. The only car on the street was an old Mercedes roadster. It looked bedraggled. Sad that someone would neglect it like that.

He walked the length of the mews, west to east, looking at each house in turn, hoping to find something that might lead to her. But there was nothing. Unsure what to do next, he turned around and retraced his steps, his shoes gradually taking on water.

18

The contractions come in waves. A breaker hits and for a terrible moment she is dragged down deep beneath the surface. She panics, convulses, gasps for air. Her muscles twist and strain. Her organs break free. Her pelvis ruptures. Her abdomen explodes. And then suddenly the Thing is out, a screaming apparition hovering above her empty belly. Born in the bed where it was conceived.

Luke takes the Thing and wraps it in a muslin cloth. He holds it close for a minute before cutting and clamping the umbilical cord. The screaming stops, and the Thing looks around the room, slowly taking possession.

Reluctantly, she takes the parcel in her arms. A revolting little piglet, with a turned-up snout and sticky red hair. And then she sees its delicate mouth, and its tiny hands, and gazes into its grey-green eyes, and it feels different. It is part of her.

At five weeks, the heart beats for the first time, though it is far too small for anyone to hear. By week six, the heart is beating 150 times per minute, the brain hemispheres are beginning to form, and brainwaves can be detected. At week seven, facial features begin to develop. In week nine, reproductive organs start to grow. By week ten, the foetus has arms and legs, fingers, and toes. After week twenty-four, it is too late to abort.

The Thing had sent the dream to torture her, but she still couldn't decide. Olga knew a quack on Harley Street who did terminations, no questions asked, provided you could pay three hundred quid in cash. But Luke had pleaded with her not to do it. He was desperate to be a father, especially father to a son. It was easy for him, though. He wouldn't have to bear the Thing for the next eight months. Or look after it, be up half the night, feeding, changing nappies, mopping up sick.

She loved her body the way it was, hers to use and abuse as she pleased. The prospect of turning into another English heifer, thighs running to fat, tits hanging like udders, filled her with horror. Added to that was the terror of turning out like her own dear mama, raising a child who'd grow up to loathe her. Motherhood held absolutely no appeal.

They'd argued and cried about it half the night. In the end she'd agreed to reconsider at week twelve. Luke said that until she passed that threshold there was no certainty that the pregnancy would be viable anyway. She might miscarry, so why not let nature take its course? It meant making the decision at Christmas. Some present. Until then everything was up in the air. And even assuming she went to term, there was no guarantee. The Thing could be stillborn.

Right now, emotionally, she felt nothing. And physically? Not much more, other than a slight bloating and a yearning for a glass of wine. Maybe she could stifle the little monster with booze and fags.

Blakey-tipped heels click-clacked loudly on the cobbles in the mews and Candy glanced out of the window. Shit! Baby brain was kicking in already. She'd forgotten to put the Merc away and it was getting soaked.

The bell rang, and thinking it was Luke she hurried downstairs to open the door. George was on the step, looking as if he'd swum ashore from a shipwreck. Why was it that you never saw a copper with a brolly? 'Evening', he said, his plump face glowing with satisfaction. 'I've got some news for you. Wanted to deliver it in person.'

He waited until they were both sitting down before making his big announcement, practically teasing the tension from the air: 'We've found your friend Margrét!'

'Well better late than never … where?'

'See if you can guess?'

'On the moon? Please George, I'm not in the mood for games.'

'She's been hiding in plain sight. It's a clever trick if you can pull it off. It was the Copenhagen connection that got me thinking. I remembered a story about two Jewish sisters there during the war. They gave the Gestapo the slip by working as waitresses in a hotel where all the Nazi officers liked to drink. The Jerries got so used to seeing the girls that they basically became invisible. So where better for Margrét to hide than in your rooms?'

'Tell me you're joking!'

'No, God's honest truth. After our trip to the morgue, I put a watch on the house, but there was nothing. Only the usual comings and goings. Then a couple of days ago I had a hunch and put the lads on round the clock and bingo! She's been letting herself in at about nine o'clock at night and leaving at seven in the morning. At first, we assumed she was just sleeping there. Then last night she came out and tapped on the window of my man's motor. Bold as brass.'

'What did she say?'

'Wanted to know if he'd like to earn some money. Said she'd seen him sitting there and suggested he make himself useful. Offered fifty quid for ten minutes' work.'

'To do what?'

'Help out with a bit of humiliation. Being an enterprising sort of chap, naturally he obliged. Went upstairs and did the business and had a quick look around while he was there. Seems like she's built up a nice little operation of her own.'

So that made Margrét the mystery intruder, using the rooms as her private playground. She must have banked on Candy not telling Olga that she'd shut up shop. In any case Olga was so used to people coming and going at all hours, that even if she'd known what Margrét was doing, she might have taken no notice.

'Who was the client: did he say?'

'I don't know. Nobody he recognised.'

'Oh well, I don't suppose it matters.'

'There's one more thing. My guy left a little gadget behind the sofa, and we picked up an interesting exchange. She must have had some other friends round later. Does "rosebud" mean anything to you?'

'It was Hearst's pet name for Marion Davies's clitoris.'

'Is that a fact? Well, some poor girl was using it as safeword. None too successfully I should add. We taped it ... I've got it with me if you want to hear it?' He took a portable cassette player from his briefcase and placed it on the table. 'The sound quality isn't great, but you'll get the general idea.'

Background noises: equipment being moved or adjusted, then a pause. *'There ... is that comfortable?'* A soft male voice. *'Thank you ... yes.'* A girl: barely audible. *'Does this hurt?'* The man's voice again.

'Oww — yes!'

'Good ...'

'OWW!'

'Did you like that?'

'I think so ...'

'Then perhaps you'll enjoy this too ...' A long pause. *'OWW! What the fuck are you doing?'* The girl again: panic evident in her voice. *'That really hurts! Let me down! ROSEBUD! ROSEBUD! ROSEBUD!'*

'Please be quiet. You're spoiling my concentration.' Then a thud, like the sound of a blunt axe hitting a log.

'That's all we've got, I'm afraid ... the tape goes silent after that. Probably a technical fault.' Candy began to shiver uncontrollably, as if her entire being resonated with the girl's suffering.

'Jesus, George, didn't you try to stop him?'

'I'd told my guy not to go in. I didn't want to upset Olga. But I phoned her this morning and brought her up to speed. She's going to change the locks. You'd better ring the bell next time you go.'

* * *

Candy ushered George in. 'Nice little set-up you've got here', he said. 'Olga does you girls proud.' He looked around appreciatively. Getting him there had been a performance, though. Eager to please as a ratter, he'd been reluctant to serve as a bloodhound. He was an armed-crime man by instinct, 'a smash-and-grab kind of guy, a quick in-and-outer'. He wasn't up for real detective work. And in any case, he'd argued, if a serious assault had been committed it was a job for the regulars, not a privateer like himself. But here they were anyway, on what George called a recce.

Seeing her rooms, Candy felt violated. A place she'd considered a sanctuary had been recast as a crime scene, to be crawled over, analysed, and picked to pieces by a hundred anonymous hands.

She showed him the black-edged card that Margrét had left for her on the mantelpiece. 'Nice', said George. 'Very thoughtful.' Then she knelt and pointed out the spots on the carpet. George scratched at the residue and dabbed it on his tongue, just as she had done. 'Definitely blood', he said, 'and these spots here look fresh.' Only then did she pick up a clue she'd missed last time: four indentations in the carpet, the telltale marks of a particular piece of equipment.

One of her clients, the Governess, liked to be restrained as though she were captive to a sadistic gynaecologist, as though there were any other kind. Rather than drill fixings into Olga's precious ceiling, Candy had commissioned a demountable stand, whose frame supported a leather sling with stirrups for the feet. When the contraption wasn't in use, it was folded up and stored in the dressing room.

It took Candy and George fifteen minutes to erect the frame and locate its feet on the carpet marks. The sling was suspended on chains, which attached to hooks at four points. When they'd finished, everything else fell into place. The blood spots corresponded exactly with the front of the sling. Ugh! One could only imagine the rest.

The sight of bloodstains set George spinning into action. Inside the flabby fetishist there were still the bones of a case-hardened copper. 'We must go to the police about this — right now!' he said. 'No excuses. No messing about.' He was on a roll: 'We've got to establish exactly what's been going on here. And you need to press charges.'

His face had turned pink with the pleasure of it all. 'I'm going to call my mate at Paddington Green. If I ask nicely, his guys shouldn't bother you too much, other than to take a statement. And if the other girls behave themselves, if you get my drift, they might even turn a blind eye to what goes on upstairs. First thing is for them to get the Forensics boffins in here and see what else they can find. Must be dabs all over the place.'

She looked around the room and groaned. There were a few special items she needed to spirit away before the boys in blue got their paws on them. And better hope the Drug Squad didn't start sniffing around too. Then they'd be in all kinds of shit. Fucking hell! Olga would be furious. She'd have to call in a whole raft of favours to get out of this little mess.

November 1984

And let's never stop shaping that society which lets each person's dreams unfold into a life of unending hope. America's best days lie ahead. And you know, you'll forgive me, I'm going to do it just one more time. You ain't seen nothin' yet!

So, the Great Discombobulator had won again. No real surprise there. Reagan was a charmer and as he had proved, charm gets you a long way. Oliver switched off the television and headed for the door.

As he mounted the steps to the Tate Gallery, he rehearsed his opening gambit: why name an avant-garde art prize after a nineteenth-century painter? He knew the curator well and wasn't looking forward to interviewing him. He affected a dishevelled air that might easily be mistaken for dim-wittedness. Lights on, nobody home, like old Ron. But whatever the question, he was always two moves ahead of you. Before they met, Oliver wanted to have a proper look at the exhibition and marshal his thoughts.

A lumpy chalk line ran along the centre of the gallery, like a rock formation brought inside the building. *Skinny oblong of knobbly geology*, he pencilled in his notebook. A piece that evoked the skeleton of a colossal spinning top, sat forlornly on the floor. Its partner, an over-sized sombrero, lay alongside. *Relics from Brobdingnagian beach party*, he wrote.

Two paintings of doubtful interest occupied one long wall: the work of the Turner winner, Malcolm Morley. *Competent technique*, he noted, unable to think of anything else. The star of the show was an exuberant photo piece by Gilbert and George. He didn't really *like* their stuff, but he admired them. They had chutzpah.

Gilbert and George should have been easy winners. They'd been cheated, really. There was talk of homophobia, but he suspected snobbery. Gilbert was a foreigner, so naturally exempt, but George was so obviously an émigré from the self-improving lower classes that it could easily have counted against him. His manners were too dainty, his demeanour too prim. You could picture him behind the counter in gentleman's outfitting, suit buttoned, lips pursed: *'Are you free Mister Passmore?' 'Yes, I'm free …'*

He'd bumped into them one evening at the little restaurant they frequented in Spitalfields. George had been flirting with the waiter, a good-looking Turkish boy, with a mop of curly black hair, but dropped him as soon as Oliver and his friends introduced themselves: trading up.

It was then that he saw her. Or at least someone who looked like her. She was wearing a chrome-yellow peacoat, with oversized buttons, and a beret pulled down asymmetrically. Without make-up she seemed younger than he remembered. 'Nola?' he called out. 'What a surprise!'

'Oh my, what a small world', she said. 'How did you even know it was me? I'm supposed to be in disguise.'

She could have sounded more enthusiastic. 'It must have been my radar …'

'This is what I look like underneath all that slap, when I've only got myself to entertain. I'm Nola's alter ego.'

'You mean like Jekyll and Hyde?'

'I suppose it's a similar story, but without the drugs and the violence.'

'Only the sex then?' he said, and she giggled.

As they walked around the room, he realised that she knew far more than he did. She was dismissive: 'I came to see what all the fuss was about, but it's just a bit of media razzamatazz. A Miss Art World contest. They'll do anything to get visitor numbers up.'

They stopped in front of Malcolm Morley's *Farewell to Crete*. Nola was captivated by the headless nude in the foreground, whose pubic bush was a forested landscape in miniature. 'I had an idea for a book a couple of years ago,' he said. 'I called it *Quim: The Vagina in Art*. I tried to persuade George Weidenfeld to publish it, but he didn't think I was serious.'

'Ha ha. I'm not sure I believe you either. But it would make a good book. I'd buy a copy.'

'Bruce said I could fill it up with art dealers, since practically all of them are cunts.'

'Correct and strategic use of the C word, I like that. But who's Bruce?'

'Bruce Chatwin. He's a friend of mine.'

'Close?'

'Not super close. We bump into each other now and then. We worked for the same company, though not at the same time. He was already a legend, and I was a lowly porter — a Sotherboy.'

'Oh, *that* company. A *Smootherboy*. Isn't working at Sotheby's more about who you know, than what you know — chatting up penniless old dukes and persuading them to flog the family silver?'

'You're probably right, but I'm afraid I never got past the first rung of the ladder.'

'I'm pleased to hear it. You know this piece isn't at all bad. It reminds me of Courbet's *L'Origine du Monde*.'

'Yes, or possibly Duchamp's *Étant donnés*.' he offered. She gave a look that translated as 'Don't get clever with me, ducky.'

'Superficially, perhaps', she said, looking at the painting with her head to one side. 'But if you think about it, you'll find they're quite different. With Courbet you're invited to share a lover's intimacy. With Duchamp there's more than a suspicion of death, as if you're looking in on a murder scene.'

'Sex and death ...' he began half-heartedly, realising he was beaten.

'The French associate the two', she interrupted. 'You know the expression *la petite mort*? It's a metaphor for orgasm.' He should have guessed that she'd be interested in erotic art. Then again, probably half the art produced in the last hundred years referenced sex in some form, so it was a broad field. But to be that knowledge-able? Nola the hostess, Nola the escort, Nola the art critic: it didn't scan. All he knew was that he found her more attractive than ever. He had an almost uncontrollable urge to kiss her on the mouth, to unbutton her coat and cup her breasts, to take her right there on the gallery floor. Now that would be an appropriate critique of the Turner Prize.

* * *

116

Back at the flat, slumped in front of the typewriter, Oliver was unable to string a sentence together without Nola creeping up and making a fool of him. How did the girl get to be so smart? Really, she had an answer for everything.

'So, you can lead a whore to culture, but you don't want her to think. Is that it?' Her words still stung. He'd assumed she must be some kind of savant, just because she was a nightclub hostess. Or, more specifically, because she was a woman with a professional interest in sex. 'But don't fret darling, three years at the Courtauld put me off art for life.' He cursed his lazy chauvinism. Obviously, she knew about art.

The phone rang, and he almost sent his glass flying in his rush to pick up: 'Nola?'

'Yes, it's me — can you be at the Park Tower at eight?'

'Of course! Where will I find you?'

'I'm in 602. Come straight up.'

20

Oliver tapped on the door. It opened silently and there she was. She had the complete Bunny outfit, perfect in every detail, right down to the collar and cuffs. A rosette on her hip announced her name. 'Good evening, sir. Welcome to the Playboy Club', she said, adopting the Bunny stance, one foot behind the other, hips squared. 'I'm your Bunny for the evening. Bunny Nola.'

'Wow, you look amazing! You didn't tell me you'd kept the costume.'

'Thank you, sir. Now what can I get you to drink?'

Damn, she was good; she was going to keep up the act. 'A scotch please, on the rocks ... and have one yourself.'

'That's very kind, but we Bunnies are forbidden to drink on duty.'

'How about off duty?'

'I'm afraid we're not allowed to drink socially with Keyholders sir.' He began to think the Bunny act might be a limiting factor. But watching her pert little tail bob up and down as she crossed the room, he rapidly changed his mind. She returned with his whisky and a menu. 'If you'd like to order dinner sir, I'll call room service.'

'Will you join me?'

'I'm afraid that won't be possible sir.'

He pulled a twenty from his wallet and tucked it into her cuff. 'Perhaps for one drink?'

'I think that will be all right, but please don't tell anyone.' He took another twenty and repeated the move. 'Perhaps another one later?'

'That would be lovely, but you won't breathe a word, will you?'

'No, I promise.'

Bunny Nola passed the menu and sat demurely on the arm of the chair — the 'Bunny perch' — while he studied it. 'How long have you been working here?' he asked, looking up.

'Oh, not long.'

'Do you enjoy it?'

'Oh yes, although the Bunny Mother is very strict. She punishes us if we step out of line.'

'Really, and how often is that?'

'Most evenings, sir.'

'I see. Has she reprimanded you tonight?'

'No, she's not here, but she left me her cane ...'

He worked the almond oil into her shoulders and down the small of her back. Her buttocks were striped with pink, and he smoothed the oil over her cheeks delicately with the palm of his hand. She flinched as he touched a particularly tender spot. 'I'm sorry ...'

'Don't apologise. It's exactly what I needed. I mean to show you my gratitude when you've finished with the oil. You've done this before, haven't you? I can tell.'

'I have a decent tennis forehand too if you're interested.'

She giggled: 'So who was your instructor?'

'I had a girlfriend at university ...'

'Go on, don't be coy. Tell me more. How did you meet her?'

'She was reading English, like me, but two years ahead. I'd seen her around quite a bit and we'd chatted a few times. Then we bumped into each other at a May Ball. We'd both arrived with other partners, but we clicked, and one thing led to another.'

'Was she your first?'

'How did you know that?'

'Just a hunch.'

'She shared a house with some other girls; but luckily, they stayed out all night. We did it all over the place. In the kitchen, on the sofa, on the stairs and eventually in bed. She said she wanted it to be memorable.'

'Sounds like my kind of girl. What was her name?'

'Dakota'

'North or south?'

'Ha ha … everyone used to say that. In fact, she was very generous in both directions. She was lovely. Dakota Ursula Koenig. Her friends called her Duck. She was a rower. Very toned, very muscly. She had long, long legs, like yours, but tiny little breasts, like little pears.'

'Did you see her again?'

'Yes, quite a bit. But she was from Boston, and she'd done her finals, so she went back to the States a few weeks later.'

'You didn't want to join her?'

'She invited me over, but I had a summer job lined up at Sotheby's, so I couldn't go straight away.'

'That doesn't sound very adventurous.'

'I know, but my grandfather had arranged it for me, so I couldn't bunk off. I didn't want to offend him.'

'But didn't you stay in touch?'

'I wrote for a while, and she sent me postcards. Then eventually I got a note saying she'd met someone. Next thing I heard she was married.'

'That's too bad. Would you turn back the clock if you could?'

'Perhaps, though I don't really believe in looking back. I always hope the best is yet to come.'

'Well, that's encouraging at least.'

'Roll over', he said, and she shifted obediently. 'Okay, now it's your turn. Tell me about your first time.'

She reached across for her bag and pulled out a pack of Gauloises Bleues: 'May I have a light?'

'Hey, aren't you supposed to be giving up?'

'I am, but I had to get into Bunny mode. I smoked like a chimney back then, and these were cool. John Lennon liked them too, so I suppose that had something to do with it. And there's a poem by Frank O'Hara — *The Day Lady Died* — do you know it?'

'No, I'm afraid I don't.'

'It's kind of elegiac, but he talks about buying Gauloises. You'll find it in *Lunch Poems*. Remind me and I'll loan it to you.'

'Thank you, I'd like that.'

'He got mown down by a dune buggy. It seems kind of prosaic, don't you think? Beat Poet as roadkill. You expect people like that to fade with dignity, from consumption, or absinthe poisoning. Or romantically, from a broken heart. Not go out with tyre marks all over them.'

'Actually, I think smoking suits you, but I can tell you're playing for time.'

'You're right, I don't know why I'm being so shy.'

'Were you very young?'

'No, I wish I could say I gave it up precociously, but I was another late starter. For some reason I was convinced I was saving myself. Heaven knows why.'

'What made you change your mind?'

'I got bored with holding out. All my friends were getting laid and talking about it all the time. So eventually I said, "fuck it". Literally.'

'Don't stop there … I want to hear the whole story.'

'I was at a party, on Boxing Day. All the loved-up girlfriends were there, performing. I must have been the only one who didn't have someone's tongue down their throat. So, I thought, fine, I'll show you. I went over to the best-looking boyfriend and said, "Take me upstairs", and he said "Now?" And I said, "Yes, and bring your friend." So that was it, start as you mean to go on.'

He massaged Nola's feet with the last of the oil, teasing it between her toes. 'Mmm, that feels good … don't stop', she said softly. 'Afterwards they said it was the best Christmas present they'd ever had. And the funniest thing was, it turned out that the precious girlfriends hadn't been putting out at all. I got the whole story. They were both little Miss Frigidaires.'

'I'm glad women have imaginary sex lives too. I assumed it was only men who talked it up like that.'

'I can assure you darling, girls fake everything!'

Nola propped herself up on the pillows and reached for the Gauloises again. She flicked her ash casually onto the carpet: another thing people only do in hotel rooms. 'It's my mother's birthday today', she said.

'Wish her many happy returns from me', he replied, unsure how the subject had come up.

'She's dead ...'

'Oh, I see ... God, I'm sorry.'

'She's been dead nearly seven years. She was forty-four, though you'd never have guessed — she was such a glamour puss.'

'What happened?'

'My father killed her ... drove his Jag into a tree on Spaniards Road and sent her flying through the windscreen.'

'No, how awful!'

'He walked away without a scratch, the bastard. Had his seatbelt on ... I got a call at the Playboy Club. I didn't have time to change, just threw a coat over my costume and ran out the door. They took her to the Royal Free but by the time I got there she was dead. They wouldn't even let me see her. She was too messed up.' She drew slowly on her cigarette. 'Stupid moron was drunk. He was always drunk. He's teetotal now though. Now that it's too late. He pretends to be in permanent mourning, but I don't believe he ever loved her. She was just a trophy. Except she was so much cleverer, and so much funnier. He had no idea what he was taking on. Nor did she really. I think she was blinded by the lifestyle.'

'Are you an only child?'

'Is it that obvious? I was a spoilt brat. A real little Jewish princess. My mother's fault, mostly. She indulged me. That's why my father sent me away to boarding school, to have some discipline beaten into me. Didn't work though, as you can see.'

'Do you take after your mother?'

'I'd like to think so, but I'm not sure. She was a nightclub hostess when they met, just like me, so I guess that must run in the family. She was quite happy when I became a Bunny, mostly because it upset my father so much. But he'd cut off my allowance, so what else was I supposed to do? You could earn a fortune in tips.'

'What made him cut you off?'

'I refused to go into therapy. It's practically a religion in Hampstead.'

'But why did he want you to see a shrink?'

'I got pregnant while I was at the Courtauld and had an abortion. I never told him that though. My mother knew. She helped me arrange it. I didn't think much about it at the time. I was just in a hurry to get it over with. But afterwards I became depressed. I was on medication. I started screwing around. I was going off the rails, getting into trouble. I think he was afraid I'd embarrass him. And then he killed her. And a week later I got fired. Everything sort of happened at once.' She paused and stubbed out her cigarette.

'Then I took the job at the Windmill. Strangely, that was when I began to enjoy life again. Most of my friends were working as secretaries or gallery girls and being paid peanuts, and I was earning the same as their bosses, just doing evenings.'

'But that was mostly tips too, right?'

'Tips and favours.'

'What kind of favours?'

'Use your imagination, darling. You're out for the night, with a wad of cash and a hard-on. What would you ask a girl to do?' The conversation was unnerving. He'd been trying to create a bubble that shut out that side of her life. 'You look miserable', she said, 'What's wrong?'

'I'm trying to work out what it is I have to do to spend more time with you, that's all.'

'That's easy. Be yourself: you're doing fine.'

'No, I mean what do I have to do to get those other guys out of your life?'

'Oh — that. I'm afraid that's much more complicated. I'm not even sure I begin to know the answer. I wish I did.'

21

From a small grey room on the fourth floor of Paddington Green Police Station, Candy looked down on the foggy ribbon of the Westway, where the rush-hour traffic had ground to its habitual standstill. She felt like death warmed up. No, warmed up and deep-fried. Morning sickness had kicked in, right on cue, as if the wretched Thing were moving ahead and making its own decisions, regardless of anything she might want.

George sat hunched in a plastic chair, a copy of the *Daily Express* in his lap, drinking sugary tea from a polystyrene cup. 'Ye gods, I hate these places!' he said. 'They all smell the same. Stale piss and floor polish.'

'How long do you think they'll keep us waiting?'

'Who knows? Probably still banging up last-night's intake ... depends how big a stick they've got.' George chortled mirthlessly at his own dismal repartee.

The door swung open, and two detectives strode in, nondescript and expressionless. 'Good morning! I'm DI Potter and this is my colleague DC Burgess. I understand you've come to make a statement, is that right?' The constable was the policewoman they'd met at the morgue.

George stuffed his paper in his jacket pocket and got up. 'Morning, Reg', he said, shaking the inspector's hand. Then turning to the constable: 'I've already explained that we want to report a crime — assault occasioning actual bodily harm.'

'And who was the victim of the assault?'

'I was', said Candy. 'But there may have been others.'

'We believe it might not have been an isolated incident. We could be looking at a continuous pattern of behaviour on the part of the assailant', said George, translating.

'Right then, let's get on with it', said the inspector. 'Please sit down. Do you mind if we tape this? It's not strictly necessary, but it often helps to have a back-up.' Candy nodded assent and the constable switched on the machine.

'This interview is being tape-recorded. I am Gaby Burgess, Detective Constable attached to Paddington Green. The other officer present is ...'

'Detective Inspector Reginald Potter, also attached to Paddington Green.'

'Date is Thursday 8th November. Time is 08.55. We are in the interview room of Paddington Green Police Station. I am interviewing ... if you could please state your full name ...'

'Candy ... I mean Catherine. Catherine Frances Fredricks.'

'Thank you. Now let's begin with the day of the assault. When was that exactly?'

'Thursday the 6th of September.'

'And where did the incident take place?'

'In the Hyde Park Hotel, Knightsbridge. Room 325.'

'And at what time did it occur, approximately?'

'It started about nine forty-five and lasted half the night.'

'Can you tell us how you were feeling that day?'

'All right, I suppose. I'd had a row on the phone with my brother-in-law the night before, so I might have been a bit unsettled. Maybe not thinking as clearly as I normally do.'

'What was the row about?'

'Is that relevant? Family stuff ...' Why were they asking her such stupid questions? And why were they taping her? She was beginning to feel as if she were the criminal.

'It doesn't matter if you don't want to elaborate. But sometimes it helps to capture feelings or emotions on the day in question. Can you describe what you did, during the course of the day, before the incident took place?'

'I spent the morning at home, doing nothing in particular; had lunch. Then in the afternoon I saw a client in my rooms. After that I went home again.'

'What time would you say you arrived home?'

'About six, maybe.'

'Then what did you do?'

'Bathed, had a glass of wine, something to eat. The usual stuff. Then I got changed ready to go out. I wore rubber that night. It takes a while to put on.'

'You say you saw a client. What sort of person would that be?'

'Male … a regular submissive. I'm a pro-domme … a professional dominatrix. I think George gave your colleague here the details.' The policewoman blushed.

'Oh, I see. Was anyone else with you during the day?'

'My maid, Margrét. She assisted me.'

'Was there anything unusual about that afternoon? Anything that stands out?'

'Only that Margrét was a bit sloppy, maybe distracted. But that didn't strike me until afterwards. Then it all began to make sense.'

'I'm sorry, I don't understand. You need to explain.'

God, this was beginning to feel as if it could take forever. 'Margrét looks after my appointments. She was the one who set me up with the guy who assaulted me. She helped him. He called himself Diessel, but I'm guessing that wasn't his real name. He was supposed to be another client, but obviously wasn't …'

The constable pulled the final sheet of paper from the typewriter and collated the pages. 'Now please read this and if you're confident it represents a true account of what happened then you can sign it.'

'Take your time', said George, reassuringly: 'There's no rush.'

She scanned the document and scribbled her name at the bottom. As stories go, it wasn't a hundred per cent complete, nor was it entirely accurate, but in terms of what happened next, she knew it made no difference. Now it was up to them.

'Look, I don't want to be over-dramatic', said George, as they waited for the lift, 'but I think you should lie low for a while. Maybe go away somewhere, take a long holiday. The Costa del Sol can be very nice at this time of year.'

It was almost funny. Melodrama was the default setting for all the coppers she knew. Anyway, she had no intention of running away. Curiosity would keep her in town if nothing else. Then there was Luke. She couldn't function without him, and there was no way he'd absent himself from the hospital. 'I don't think so', she said. 'I plan to stick around.'

22

Oliver decided at the last minute to take Nola to see *Don Giovanni*. It was a matinée performance at Covent Garden and with luck she'd been free that afternoon. It was dark by the time they left the theatre, and the paving stones glistened with a fresh covering of ice. Oliver wound his scarf up tightly.

'Do you have time for a coffee?' he asked, 'There's a little place I know not far from here.'

'Sure', said Nola, linking arms, 'I'm all yours.'

'Thomas Allen made a convincing Don, don't you think?'

'Yes ... sexy but dangerous. Exactly the right mix.'

'But Mozart should have wrapped it up when the Commendatore comes for the Don, don't you agree? It should have been a cliff-hanger. Does good prevail over evil, does the Devil get him or not?'

'You're right. It's the director's cut thing', she said. 'Can you imagine Mozart in Hollywood? *Sorry Mo, you gotta lose fifteen minutes.* If I were directing, I'd cast the Don as a woman ... *Donna Giovanna.* That would give it an edge, don't you agree?'

'Isn't that the Lulu story?'

'I suppose so, but it must be due for a remake.'

'It probably is, but your Donna would meet damnation much faster than the Don.'

'You think so?'

'Absolutely! There's no way she'd be allowed to enjoy life for nearly so long.'

The coffee shop was small and snug, with bare floorboards and wooden pews, like a Nonconformist chapel let off the leash. People had gravitated towards the warmth at the back of the shop and Oliver and Nola had to make do with seats by the door. They had barely sat down when Liza came in and began to study the selection of coffees chalked up behind the counter. 'Hello!' he said, touching her arm, 'What a coincidence.'

'Oh hi! I didn't see you … I'm sorry I don't remember your name.'

'It's Oliver. And this is …'

'We've met', said Nola.

'Silly me', he said, 'I'd forgotten about the club.'

'I haven't seen you there for a while though, Oliver, have I?' said Liza, 'A pity, we could do with a few more good-looking boys.' Her eyes smiled.

'So, what brings you here?' he asked.

'Well, funnily enough I came to buy some coffee.'

'No, I meant geographically.'

'Oh, I see, ha ha. I'm on my way home. My studio's upstairs. Why don't you come up when you've finished? It's the green door on your left as you come out. Just ring the bell.'

He glanced at Nola, and she nodded. 'Okay, we'll see you in a while.'

The faint clink of crockery and the muted hiss of the espresso machine intruded into Liza's studio from below. The room was bare, apart from a long table, on which she explained that she did the cutting and gluing. Beneath it were rolls of rubber sheeting in maybe a dozen different colours. Finally, he located the mysterious scent he'd been unable to identify at Maitresse.

'I put that on for you', said Liza, pointing to a fan heater. 'I generally keep it cold in here. It makes the material easier to work.' She showed them the little tool with a rotating blade that she used to cut the rubber. Among the offcuts was a small label that read *Liza Gray — Latex Couture*.

'What are you making at the moment?' he asked.

'I finished this today', she said, turning a mannequin around.

It was a calf-length red rubber dress, scooped and laced across at the back. 'It's for Siouxsie Sioux — she's coming by later to pick it up.'

He wasn't really listening. 'You look terrific', he said.

'Thank you. I always try to wear something I've made myself, though people can sometimes be a bit weird about rubber.'

Liza wasn't beautiful exactly, but she was magnetic. She was wearing a fluffy primrose sweater over a knee-length rubber skirt. The skirt was tight but had a pleat at the back, like a fishtail, which quivered as she moved. He wasn't sure which was the more arousing, the softness of the angora or the sheen of the latex. Jesus, he was turning into Ed Wood.

Back in the street, Nola took his hand gently, as if to kiss it, then sank her teeth into the fleshy bit below the thumb. 'Ow! ... What have I done to deserve that?'

'Your eyes were practically on stalks, you rat! And who knows where your tongue was heading. Just for that you can drive me home. And then that's it for today. I've got to work tonight.'

They found the car shimmering with frost, its windscreen a budding polar landscape. Oliver spotted a fresh scrape in its silver paintwork and winced. Every scratch was like a wound.

'This is a sexy little machine', said Nola.

'I'm glad you like it. It's a 356. I squandered half my savings on it a few years ago, but I'm beginning to think I should get rid of it.'

'Why? It suits you.'

'It's not the car that's the problem. It's the brand. You see so many City boys poncing about in their fat-arsed 911s that no right-thinking person wants to drive a Porsche these days.'

'I know nothing about cars. But you shouldn't be so concerned about what people think. It will only feed your inhibitions.'

The doors opened with an unfamiliar crackle. Now would it start? He set the choke and turned the key, holding it until to his great relief the engine struggled noisily to life. Then he diverted air from the puny little heater up onto the screen. 'Apologies for the technical shortcomings', he said. 'It will warm up in a minute or two.'

They sped along Strand into Fleet Street, towards the mute fortress of the *Telegraph* and the Black Lubyanka of the *Daily Express*. The stream of journalists from El Vino signalled that the early editions were going to press.

'Isn't this your territory?' she asked.

'Yes ... better not knock anyone down. They'll be so full of alcohol by now, they'll spontaneously combust.' Nola giggled and he accelerated rapidly away from the lights, up Ludgate Hill and on towards St Paul's. Past the churchyard, he swung north. A glimpse of London Wall revealed an alien townscape of office slabs, its architecture utterly commodified and degraded. If Roland Barthes was right, to find man's highest artistic achievements one must no longer look to architects but to car designers. Ergo: there is no Granada of our age, only Ford Granadas. A depressing prospect.

Nola gave directions for the final leg. They stopped at the foot of one of the Barbican towers, a concrete behemoth that looked as if an artillery emplacement had been extruded through forty storeys, then glazed in. She leaned across and pecked his cheek.

'I was going to suggest another date', he said.

'I'd be disappointed if you didn't. I've got lots more surprises in store when I let you out of the doghouse.'

'I know it's short notice, but I'll be in New York next week for the *Telegraph* and I might stop over for a few days. We could have the weekend together.'

She paused long enough for his heart to sink. 'I don't know; that could be difficult. I have things to do.'

'I should have given you more warning, I know. But they only asked me yesterday. It could be fun ... will you think about it?'

She leant forward and kissed him again, then squeezed his arm affectionately. 'Let me see. No promises.'

As Oliver drove home, Don Giovanni bothered him more and more. *Ma in Ispagna ... Mille e tre! Mille e tre!* One thousand and three. Could that really be possible?

In his cups after supper, Bruce had produced a *New York Times* cutting he kept in the back of his notebook and quoted an astonishing statistic. Someone had calculated that a gay man suffering from AIDS would typically have had 1,160 sexual partners. Bruce hadn't volunteered his own score, but even half that number was incredible. Even a quarter. In any case, how could you possibly be sure without a Leporello on hand to keep the tally?

His personal count was far easier since there were so few. Nola was number sixteen. At his present rate of progress, it would be another ten years before he met number thirty-two. And his libido probably wouldn't last the course anyway. Before he reached sixty-four, the beast would have slipped its chains.

23

'Mr Johnson can give you thirty minutes at two o'clock', said the secretary. 'Please be punctual Mr Woolf, he has a busy calendar.' Naively, he'd assumed lunch at the Four Seasons, or perhaps cocktails somewhere, but clearly the *Telegraph* didn't quite cut it. Johnson was an architect as nurtured in the imagination of Ayn Rand, born to succeed by bending in the wind of every prevailing style.

In the flesh, he was tall and lean, with a mottled scull. Predatory eyes glinted behind trademark spectacles, giving him a raptor-like air. His room was unexpectedly austere. No pictures or photographs, and his desk was bare, apart from a roll of yellow trace and a pot of pencils. The view, though, was sublime — down to the East River and across to Queens.

He'd been to see Johnson's new AT&T tower on Madison Avenue. It looked like a giant tallboy. Fifty years ago, nobody would have given it a second glance, but that wasn't the issue. It had so upset the Modernist old guard, of which Johnson had once been the darling, that it had become a major news story.

'I think it's a good building, Mr Johnson', Oliver said, holding out his hand. 'And at your age you're entitled to some fun.'

The old man's expression suggested he'd swallowed a lemon. 'I've had fun all my life, young man!' he spat back. Clearly it was going to be a difficult half hour.

'Siddown, siddown ...'

Oliver opened his notebook and lobbed out a question. 'So, how should we interpret the shift from Modern to Postmodern in your work — what does it say about the future direction of architecture?'

'Damned if I know.'

Correction: a very difficult half hour. 'Let me put it another way: how did you come to design a Postmodern building ... to build in stone instead of steel?'

'It's what they wanted.'

'You mean if they'd asked for a building like this one, you'd have done that instead?'

'Sure, why not?'

'You wouldn't try to persuade them to do something different.'

'No, why should I? Listen, everybody wants a happy client. Architects are pretty much high-class whores. We can turn someone away if we don't like the look of them, same as they can. But if we want to stay in business, we gotta say yes pretty regularly. And you don't say no to American Telephone and Telegraph.'

He'd heard that schtick a million times, so went on the attack. 'Mr Johnson, you are on record as saying "What good does it do to believe in beautiful things? It's much better to be nihilistic and forget all that." What exactly did you mean?'

'Well, that was a long time ago.'

'You wouldn't say that now?'

'No. That is, yes. What I was trying to say was that the public has lost its passion for greatness. Look at Grand Central. You can stop them tearing it down, but you can't make them love it. They have the finest space in the city, and they let Kodak ruin it with their advertising. You know what I'm talking about? The goddam Coloramas! Last time I went through, there were fifteen giant babies overhead, 'bout nine feet high. People don't care for grandeur any longer. They just want value for money.'

'You mean they're more interested in the bottom line than the skyline.'

'That's exactly what I mean! Happens that with AT&T the

131

bottom line was set high, and the skyline came cheap. That pediment cost nothing compared with their marketing spend. So, it works for everyone.'

* * *

'A scotch on the rocks, sir?' Boy, he needed it. 'Thank you ... a large one.' Algonquin waiters were the best. He took a slug of the Macallan and read through his notes. The old buzzard had given him nothing. Architects were all the same, always regurgitating the same old lines.

After Johnson ejected him, he'd headed down to Grand Central to look at the Colorama. Sadly, he'd missed the babies — they were running a Christmas photograph. Did it compromise the space? Not really. You may as well complain that the thousands of people who rush through the concourse every day spoilt its purity; or that decades of cigarette smoke had given the ceiling a patina of soot. But architecture isn't like sculpture. It gets lived in, and sometimes it gets a little messy. The genius lies in being able to anticipate and contain that mess. Grand Central achieved that effortlessly. Johnson's tragedy was that he couldn't see it. But then perhaps most architects were like that? And maybe there was a lesson there for him too? Even a well-ordered life generates its own chaos.

Over breakfast, he planned the morning's expedition. He wanted to visit the Cedar Tavern. There was nothing special about the place itself. It was a crummy neighbourhood bar. But as a second home to some of the city's greatest artists and writers, it had gained an aura. If you'd gone there virtually any night in the early Fifties, you'd have found Jackson Pollock high on Duco, or Robert Motherwell holding court. Stories of misbehaviour were legion. Pollock had been barred for ripping the men's room door off its hinges. Ditto Jack Kerouac, for pissing in the sink. He pictured a long zinc-topped bar along one side of a narrow space, with booths at the back, the walls a hospital green, a neon sign flickering. He wanted to order a beer on the spot where Willem de Kooning and Mark Rothko, Frank

O'Hara and Allen Ginsberg had drunk, and take it all in.

On his way out, he paused at the reception desk.

'Good morning, Mr Woolf.'

'Hi, er, good morning', he said. 'Are there any messages for me?'

'One, sir ... a lady called. She said to meet her in Central Park this afternoon at three. She'll be waiting by the Sherman Monument.'

'Did she leave her name?'

'A Miss Nola sir ...'

So, she'd made it after all.

He knew he was in love with her. He also knew that she would soon tire of him. All he wanted was to ride the wave for as long as possible, even if he was left clinging to the emotional wreckage when, finally, it came crashing down.

He strode on, automatically. The route downtown was so familiar that he tuned out the architecture entirely. Buildings that once thrilled receded into the background. But the Flatiron stopped him in his tracks. Everybody knows the building for its prow, but walk around and approach it from behind, as he did now, and you find something entirely different — an extruded Renaissance palazzo. There was Johnson's AT&T! All the old crook had done was launder it and give it a funny hat. Duchamp said that all art was either plagiarism or revolution, and so it was with architecture. He was happy: he had a hook.

Just as he feared, he arrived at the Cedar to find no bar there. The entire block had disappeared beneath a new apartment building, and a Levi's store traded where Kerouac once stood. He felt like a stupid literary tourist.

He'd suffered a similar humiliation in Paris. As a student, tracing Hemingway's footsteps, he'd sought out a table in Brasserie Lipp and ordered a beer and *pommes* à *l'huile* with a serving of *cervelas*, as the master describes in *A Moveable Feast*. But instead of recognising an aficionado, they clearly couldn't wait to get rid of him. Nowadays, even Hemingway would be ejected as a pauper.

Well, if you look like a tourist and feel like a tourist, what the hell: why not behave like one? He shaded his eyes and gazed up at the silvery peaks of the World Trade Center towers.

Windows on the World was exactly that. He sat at a table on the 106th floor, gazing out north along the island. The towers cast rapier shadows that continued forever along the Hudson foreshore. Everything else was so small — the Empire State reduced to a toy, the spire of the Chrysler thinned to a hypodermic needle, the liners at the piers looking as if they might bob about in your bath. He understood how the first balloonists must have been thrilled by the sight of cities from the air. The perception of space and scale was entirely novel. He looked out, utterly transfixed.

The waiter brought a dozen Moonstone oysters and a half-bottle of Laurent-Perrier. The champagne sparkled and soothed. The first oyster was as fresh and invigorating as an Atlantic rock pool; the second brought the prospect of the sea to his lips; and the third rekindled a memory of that first night with Nola. He ate the others slowly, savouring the salty flesh. But satisfaction soon ceded to melancholia. He lit a cigarette and opened his book. Since Nola introduced him to Frank O'Hara, he'd been consuming his work, as if trying to find his way into another part of her:

Why should I share you? ...
I am the least difficult of men.
All I want is boundless love.

Had O'Hara known someone like Nola? What more was there to be said?

* * *

Sherman's beckoning statue glowed fiery gold. Sherman, the man who burned Atlanta. He spotted Nola from maybe half a block away. In her winter coat and mink hat, she could have been Anna Karenina waiting on the platform of the Moscow station. Close up, she was pink-cheeked and aristocratic. He kissed her quickly on the mouth. 'Hello stranger, when did you get in?'

'Yesterday evening', she said, not entirely convincingly.

'Oh, you should have called. We could have had dinner.'

'I know, but I wanted to see an old friend and Thursday is her only night off.' I'm here at your invitation, but you don't own my time was the obvious subtext.

'What does she do, or shouldn't I ask?'

'She's called Irina and she works in a bar ... the Red Wedge. Do you know it?'

'No, but we could drop in later. Where is it?'

'Downtown. All the Wall Street Big Dicks go there after work. Then when they head off to wherever Masters of the Universe live, a different crowd comes in. That's the time to go.'

'Okay, let's do it', he said, trying to sound a little more upbeat. 'So where are you staying?'

'The St Regis.'

'That sounds expensive.'

'It is, but they do things properly there. I think you'll like it. It's where they invented your Bloody Mary.'

'It sounds like the perfect place to have breakfast.'

'Don't worry darling, you're invited. Come, let's take a walk ...'

They followed the path as it edged the pond. Ahead of them on the bridge an old lady in furs was tossing bread to a gaggle of geese. *'I was wondering where the ducks went when the lagoon got all icy and frozen over ...'*

'Isn't that Holden Caulfield?' he said.

'Yes, inspired by this very spot.'

Curiously, he preferred the park in winter. The trees in their nakedness assumed an abstract sculptural quality, as if they'd been reconceived by Giacometti. And when the snow settled and the frost formed, the monochrome effect was quite beautiful. It took him back in time, to images of skaters with scarves and mufflers, darting around on frozen lakes.

'I've never been here before', she said. 'I was always told it was too dangerous.'

'I suppose it was until recently. But then so was the entire city.

135

Did you know that Olmsted used as much dynamite to create the park as was expended during the Battle of Gettysburg?'

'Really? That's one of the things I love about you Oliver, you're a minefield of useful information.'

He chose to ignore her. 'And the incredible thing is that it was being done at more or less the same time. They would have been blasting this landscape into existence while the Civil War was raging less than two hundred miles away. It gives you a sense of how incredibly confident they must have been about the future.'

'They were giants then. We're pygmies now', she said.

'I know. I sometimes look at places like this and find it terribly dispiriting. We wouldn't know where to begin to make something so beautiful and on such a scale.'

'You're right. It's really the world's biggest work of art. The rest of the island is merely an elaborate frame.'

'Isn't that the Dakota building?' Nola asked, pointing. 'I think it's creepy. I wouldn't want to live there, no matter how good the view.'

'They say Boris Karloff kept a flat in the attic, but then I suppose you'd have to in his position.'

He used to tease his own lovely Dakota that he enjoyed her so much, he was going to take up permanent residence. He was a fool. He should have seized the moment, got on a plane, gone after her, proposed, or whatever it was she wanted. But at the time, she was just the first notch on the bedpost. How was he to know that a girl like her comes along maybe once in a lifetime, if at all. Maybe she missed him too. Did she wake in the morning and contemplate finding him, as he did her?

He wished he was a passionate being, that for once in his life he could be reckless, live in the moment; but he was cold-blooded, cautious, risk averse. That's how he lost her and most likely how he'd lose Nola too. He glanced at his watch. 'We can walk by the Dakota if you like', he said, 'we've got plenty of time.'

Close to the entrance, near where Lennon fell, someone had left a white rose. 'I think that's mawkish', he said. 'You see floral tributes everywhere these days. Run over a dog and some idiot will leave flowers.'

136

'Actually, I think it's touching … a white rose symbolises regret.'

They stood there for a moment, looking through the big iron gates into the courtyard.

'We're back to Holden Caulfield', he said. 'Mark Chapman had this weird thing about him.'

A Japanese girl knelt and placed a scrappy arrangement of yellow daisies, the kind of thing you'd buy in a drugstore. 'The first of many', said Nola, when the girl had gone. 'It's Lennon's anniversary soon. There'll be a vigil here.'

'Let's go', he said. 'Not sure I'm ready for the Second Coming.'

A cab stopped to let a couple out and Oliver stepped forward: 'The St Regis', he said, holding the door open for Nola, then climbing in after her.

'Actually, you can see why Lennon offended a religious nut like Chapman', she said as the cab pulled away. 'I think he really did have a thing about being a Christ figure. The hair and the beard were all part of it.'

'You mean the Hair Peace, Bed Peace scene?'

'Yes, with Yoko channelling Mary Magdalene.'

'No, Lennon was a prankster. While the rest of the world was staging sit-ins, he decided to have a lie-in.'

'Wasn't Hair Peace a pun — hair piece?'

'Try saying it with a Liverpool accent', he said. Nola looked puzzled. 'Go on — imagine you're a Liver Bird, waiting on the pierhead. You have to say it aloud though, otherwise you won't get it.'

'Her peas … *herpes*!'

She let out a shriek that caught the driver right in the ear. The guy swerved and cursed: 'Jeezus, lady!'

'You mean all this time nobody's picked it up?'

'No! Isn't it hilarious? Everyone thinks he was some kind of messiah. But he was just a very naughty boy.'

'He was beautiful though. What they did to him makes me cry.'

* * *

The Red Wedge occupied a space like a railroad car, extruded from a frontage no more than ten feet wide. A red leather banquette ran the length of one wall, and a bar counter occupied the other side. Spotlights illuminated groups of drinkers at random; everything else was lost in darkness.

A Slavic-looking girl emerged, apparently from nowhere, carrying a tray laden with glasses. The raven hair, the powdered face, the crimson lips, the big black eyes, everything about her spelled witch not waitress.

'This is Irina', said Nola. 'Irina ... Oliver.'

'I didn't expect to see you this evening', Irina said and blew Nola a kiss. 'Pleased to meet you, Oliver. Nola's told me all about you.' Nola shot her a look and Irina winked. 'Are you guys happy at the bar, or would you like a table?'

'No, I think we're fine here for a while', he replied: 'So how do you two know each other?'

'We escaped the clutches of the Evil Empire together', said Nola.

'She means the Playboy Club', said Irina.

'We were co-conspirators', said Nola. 'The two Bad Bunnies. Irina was my guide in all things forbidden by management, of which there were quite a few. The naughty girl schlepped all the way from Moscow to lead me astray, didn't you darling? We were always getting into mischief. But she's much smarter than me, so never got caught.'

'I jumped before I was pushed', said Irina. Nola was animated. Irina was cool, content to stand there and let them orbit around her.

'And it was clever Irina who rescued my Bunny costume for me, so you have her to thank for that', said Nola. 'Sometimes I think that naughty little rabbit has a sex life of its own. I must remember to look under its tail when I get home.'

Arranged on glass shelves above the bar was a seemingly limitless assortment of vodkas. Miscellaneous other bottles were relegated to the counter below. He watched entranced as Irina cut a perfect curl of lemon peel and placed it on the rim of a glass. Oof, the way she flicked that knife.

'What can I get you, Oliver?' Irina asked.

'I don't know, I'm not a big vodka drinker … What do you recommend?'

'Well let me see. How about a Pornstar? Or a Slow Screw?' Bloody hell, it must be written all over his face. 'Or maybe you'd like to try a White Russian?' Irina continued, 'Nola will, I'm sure.' He looked at Nola, hoping he was wrong.

'Darling, even in this light I can tell you're blushing', Nola said. 'But I think you'll find that they're all quite yucky. Stick with a martini. Four and you can be under the hostess.'

24

His mouth was dry, his tongue had thorns, and his brain was trying to pop his eyeballs out. He couldn't remember ever being this feeble. In fact, he didn't remember much at all: an avalanche of cocaine and now a mental whiteout. He padded to the bathroom and filled a glass with water. He needed an aspirin, but there were none. Perhaps he should lie in the bath for a while and soak his desiccated body back into shape? No, he closed the door quietly and turned on the shower.

'Ollie?' He heard her calling from the bedroom. 'Ollie, where are you? Come back to bed.' He reached for a towel. 'I'm in here!'

'Hello handsome', she said, appearing in the doorway. 'I wondered where you'd disappeared to.' Then she surveyed the scene and was suddenly business-like. 'We should clean this mess up. We don't want to advertise the fact that Charlie was here last night.' She ran a finger along the counter and dabbed the powder on her tongue: 'Yum, shame to waste it. You know someone calculated that ninety per cent of all the hundred-dollar bills in this city have seen Charlie at some point. Nothing but the best for Ben Franklin.'

'That's probably only because the rest haven't been unwrapped', he said, still barely functioning: 'I have the most appalling headache. I'm not sure whether it was the vodka or the coke … I'm not used to either.'

'Poor boy, you've lived such a sheltered life.'

'It's true. And you've corrupted me.'

'That's good. I like to think we're stretching your boundaries. Come, let's stretch them a little more. I promise to be gentle with you.'

* * *

Saturday brunch in the Astor Court was practically a Manhattan institution. Nola ordered scrambled eggs and Bloody Marys for them both — a 'Red Snapper' they called it — and a pot of coffee. 'Eggs are the best thing for a hangover', she said. 'You'll soon pick up.'

'This place was once the city's social hub', he said, surveying the room. 'It's hard to believe that now though. Look at this crew. Old Mrs Astor would be mortified.'

'You can't tell these days. Americans all dress like six-year-olds at the weekend, even the millionaires.'

'You know, the Astors probably dined with the Fricks in this room. And the Carnegies and the Rockefellers. If it weren't for the horde, you could almost cast yourself back to the Gilded Age ...'

The conversation was forced, brittle: so ridiculously *English*. Neither of them wanted to talk about Irina or the genie she'd set free during the night. When the Red Wedge closed, they'd taken a cab back to the St Regis and gone straight up to Nola's room. He'd poured them drinks while she got ready for bed; unusually hesitantly, he now realised. They hadn't been in the room long when there was a tap-tap on the door. It was Irina, who else?

'I've brought some things for the party', she said, patting her bag. Nola had helped her with her coat and then, without prompting, begun to undress her. Irina's body was lean and muscly, almost mannish. Entranced by the performance at the time, he realised that he'd been privy to a well-practised routine. Nola really did like a White Russian.

'Tell me Oliver', Irina had asked, 'are you a top or a bottom?' It was Alice's question again: *what turns you on?* He'd said, 'I like to keep an open mind', or something idiotic like that, but she hadn't

140

been impressed: 'My guess is you're a bottom. As is Nola, which is why the two of you need a dom like me. Now get your lazy English butt over here!'

He'd sensed Nola watching them. 'Save some for me', she'd said, touching his shoulder. She'd been alert and refreshed — her friend Charlie again. He hated it that she'd gone down on Irina so enthusiastically, and that they'd both enjoyed it so much. Nola's quim should have been his prerogative.

Irina had cut lines for them, and they'd done coke with Quaalude chasers to give a lift during the come down. Who knows how much they'd got through. Enough to kill Elvis. 'Medicate to fornicate', Irina said. But boy, she forgot to mention the hangover. And then there was her bag of tricks, a cornucopia of sex toys. He had no idea that anyone could be so well accessorised. Or use them so effectively.

Nola was spellbound, and he understood why. Irina made mischief seem irresistible. That accent was mesmerising. And those eyes. Like the deepest, darkest wells imaginable. Endless reserves of devilment. You could tumble in and be lost forever.

Nola lit yet another cigarette. She was earwigging on the geriatrics at the next table, probably trying to gauge their net worth. But what else was going through her mind? Could she tell how much he'd enjoyed last night and how much he wanted to do it again, with her, with anyone? Almost certainly — the girl could see round corners.

His grandfather used to joke that he was *buy sexual*: 'I've had many women, professional and otherwise, and on the whole professional is cheaper.' The old goat thought it was hilarious. But it wasn't so amusing to find yourself longing for a woman and yet knowing that you could never be satisfied by her alone. Last night's evidence pointed Nola in a similar direction. So where did that leave them? A bisexual couple. Surely not a first. But what were the chances of that lasting? And since he was confronting his demons, he should face the truth about the blessed Dakota. He'd confided in her one night and she'd humiliated him.

'Where I come from, honey, men are men', she said. 'You better decide whose team you're on.'

Ugh! He drained his glass and signalled to the waiter for another Bloody Mary.

25

Midnight in Rockefeller Plaza. The Christmas lights sparkled, but the ice rink was silent, its skaters long gone. Oliver sat and contemplated the statue of Prometheus, reduced to a gilded bauble beneath the mighty Rockefeller tree. He kept coming back to Bruce and their conversation in the library. Prometheus had been condemned to be chained to a rock and have his liver eaten by an eagle, only for it to regenerate overnight and the process to begin again at dawn: immortality as living hell. Abandoned and miserable, he wanted to empathise, but instead his insignificance welled up and washed right over him.

He'd hoped to spend a second night with Nola, but after dinner she'd packed him off to the Algonquin. He knew there would be someone else in her bed. Male or female, it didn't seem to matter. He reached for his Gauloises, Nola's influence again, and stared at the pack, momentarily baffled. Wrapped around it was an unfamiliar piece of paper. He unfolded it and read:

New York's ONLY *true Underground Club beneath the city streets! … Fulfil your deepest & darkest desires at the* HELLFIRE

Turning the paper over he saw Nola's note: *Go — Irina will be there to look after you!*

* * *

RELAX DON'T DO IT, WHEN YOU WANT TO COME …

'Sorry, would you mind turning that thing down?' The monstrous wall of sound receded, and Oliver pulled the cab door shut. 'Thank you! That's much better.'

'Where to Mister?'

'Ninth at West 14th please.'

'Okay … but you sure you wanna go down there?'

'Why, what's the problem?'

'Can be kinda dangerous if you don' know your way round.'

'I'm meeting a friend', he said. 'I'll be fine — it's twenty-eight on Ninth.'

'Yeah, I know it. The Hellfire. You sure you really wanna go?'

'Look, just drive! Okay?'

'No need to get upset Mister!' The guy hit the gas and turned the music up, way beyond the pain threshold.

A bitter wind cut in off the Hudson to attack him, coiling around his neck and stinging his eyes. He looked up and down the street, expecting to see a neon logo. But the only sign of life was a bulb above a staircase that led down to a cellar. The stair was caged in with steel mesh, its gate chained open. It had to be the Hellfire. The only other place he'd seen anything like it was on the Falls Road, in Belfast, where trouble regularly came a calling.

At the foot of the stairs, he confronted a featureless sheet of rusting metal. It was sealed tight, and he hunted in the half-light for a handle or a buzzer.

'Just bang on it', said a voice, the Brooklyn accent sawing through the air. 'They always open up.'

He turned to see a couple of heavies in biker gear at the top of the stairs. He slapped the door hard, as instructed, and it swung open.

'Yeah, who's there?'

'Oliver Woolf'

'You know it's members only, right?'

'Irina invited me.'

'Irina who?'

'Russian Irina.'

'Okay. Ten bucks!'

Oliver handed over the cash and the Brooklyn leathermen followed him in.

The vault was darker than the street and smelt damp and earthy. Heavy metal thudded and pounded, the acoustics stifling everything but the base. Couples conjoined; figures squatted in cages; depravity overlaid debauchery. It was the Devil's dance-hall. Hieronymus Bosch's *Garden of Earthly Delights* come to life. Where else but New York City?

He negotiated his way towards the light of the bar and the promise of alcohol. The bar top was an immense length of mahogany that must have started life in some long-lost gin palace. Midway along, a girl lashed to a giant lazy Susan was being pleasured half-heartedly by the barman. Both were naked and aggressively hirsute.

'A Bud please', Oliver said, regretting that he'd interrupted the performance. The guy spat on the floor and spun the girl around.

'You'd like a piece of that too, wouldn't you, hun?' said a familiar voice behind him. 'Just ask Chuck here ... Hairy Mary is his property. He keeps the naughty little pussy close, so she can't stray.'

'Irina! Nola said I'd find you here.'

'Welcome! But are you sure you've got the right address?' she asked, tugging at his jacket. 'You look like you've come straight from business school.'

'I know', he said, 'But I'm really not kitted out for this scene.'

Irina, on the other hand, was dressed to kill. Her leather catsuit was unzipped to the navel and a studded belt hung loosely on her hips. A rouged nipple said, 'look at me', but a horse whip said, 'don't touch'.

'I think we'd better find something to help you blend in', she said. 'Come with me!'

He followed her into a coalhole of a room at the back of the club. 'This is Jerry's office', she said. 'He usually keeps a bunch of stuff in here that people have left behind.' She rooted around and pulled a box from beneath a beaten-up steel desk. The desktop itself was almost a work of art. Hundreds of names and telephone numbers had been scratched into its navy-grey paint, as if Cy Twombly had been tasked to transcribe a Rolodex. In the middle of the composition someone had inscribed the solitary word *KUNT* in an illiterate script.

Irina pulled things from the box until she found what she was looking for. 'Here try this on ... it looks about your size', she said, holding up a rubber T-shirt.

He slipped off his jacket and sweater and tugged his shirt over his head. The T-shirt was cold and clammy. The matt material stuck to itself, and Irina had to come to his aid, easing the shirt over his shoulders and smoothing it down his back. She loosened the belt on his jeans and tucked in the tail.

'There, that's perfect', she said, patting his bottom. 'Now all you need is buffing up.' She took an aerosol can from the desk drawer and shook it: 'Close your eyes … silicone spray. No rubber-ist should be without it. Guaranteed to make you shine!'

'It suits you', she said, when she'd finished. 'I can't believe you haven't tried it before.'

'It's been rather a weekend of firsts', he replied.

'Glad to hear it. Hope that journey's been enjoyable. Now I think it's time we called on Mr C.' She reached into the back of the drawer and pulled out an ancient tobacco tin, a surprisingly delicate piece, with a red disc imposed on a pale blue-and-gold ground. She turned it over in her hand, as if judging its value, then flipped it open. 'Jerry always keeps a stash of the good stuff here somewhere. You have to know where to look.'

'You seem to know your way around pretty well.'

'I should do. I work here most weekends. I like it. Jerry keeps the door tight to weed out the gawkers and the B&Ts. It means we can relax and not worry who's looking.'

She cut two lines out on the desktop and passed the furled fifty that Jerry kept in the tin. 'Here, after you …'

The cocaine wrought its unerring magic: the white stuff. His heartbeat rose to meet the new-found rhythm of the music; he grew leaner, stronger; his muscles rippled beneath their glossy new skin. He was hungry, predatory, unbound.

'Now let's go see what we can find you to play with', Irina said. 'It's time you were blooded properly.'

Two blondes, stripped bare, were shackled to one of the columns that marched through the space. *Chain Me!* demanded the lipstick scrawl on the stomach of one; *Whip Me!* exhorted the script on the other.

'They tell people they're twins, but they're not even sisters', said Irina, prodding Miss Chain Me! in the belly with her whip. 'Just kissin' cousins ... a couple of Okie corn dolls. They breed them all the same down there. I call them Tweedledum and Tweedledee.'

'Then they should say *Eat Me!* and *Drink Me!*'

'Now you're getting into the party spirit!' she cried, delighted. 'Atta boy! You can have them one at a time, or both together. And if you can't manage them in one go, just ask for a doggie bag and you can finish them off at home!'

Oliver leaned against the bar, nursing a beer and a deflated ego. Once, when he'd been falling behind in his second year at Cambridge, a period of experimentation in all kinds of ways, his father had admonished him: 'Be careful my boy, you are becoming a Bohemian!'

Well, if the old man could see him now. Charlie's beneficent high had been relatively short-lived and his fall back to earth more wretched than before. He would have pulled out his fingernails for a Quaalude to float his boat again. But something more potent was required to keep the adrenaline flowing. He needed another fix of the deeply addictive wonder drug called Nola.

At that moment he was consumed by the thought of her lying between soft sheets in the St Regis, her body being explored by a nameless usurper. He should have been up there, in heaven, but here he was at the opposite extreme.

'Hello lover boy! Did you manage both courses?'

'Oh, hi', he said, looking up at Irina. 'No, not quite. I lost my appetite.'

'Do you need a pick-me-up? There's plenty more C to be had...'

'You know, I think I should go home. I feel done in.'

'No! The night's still young and you haven't met any of my friends yet.'

'Look, I'm sorry ...'

'Oh, wait ... here's Jerry', said Irina, introducing a thick-set dude. Another big believer in hair, he had a spade beard about a foot long. 'Jerry runs this place. There's nothing he hasn't seen ... or done.'

'Pleased to meet you', said Jerry. 'Enjoy!'

There was something familiar about Jerry, but he struggled to make the connection. His brain was so addled you could practically hear the synapses trying to connect. Then finally a spark: Jerry was another of the faces from Mapplethorpe's Hellfire series. Candy's portrait had set him on the trail, and he'd found more of them in an old exhibition catalogue.

'A girl I know used to come here', Oliver said. 'She's called Candy … Mapplethorpe photographed her. Does the name mean anything to you?'

'Yeah, it might. You know Mapplethorpe?'

'No, he's a friend of a friend, but we've never met.'

'Didn't think so. You don't look the part. He took a shine to Candy though. Matter of fact, she was here in the summer. But she used to be a regular, way back. Used to hang out with a guy who does tattoos, over on A Street. She's a kinky little minx. Seen her busy here many a time!'

Oliver recoiled, notwithstanding his own form as a voyeur. 'When was she here exactly … do you happen to recall the date?'

'No, 'fraid I don't. What happened t' her, she still livin' in the city?'

'No, she's in London now. That's how we met.'

'Well tell her Jerry says hello. So, who's your friend?'

'Sorry, what friend?'

'The Mapplethorpe connection.'

'Oh, I see. Bruce Chatwin … he seems to know everyone.' *Collect* everyone would have been more accurate. Bruce was such a snob, always going on about 'provenance'. Oliver's allusion to his own literary ancestry had been enough to secure a place in Bruce's circle. Though ever the auctioneer, Bruce hadn't bothered to check. If he had, he'd have discovered that his branch of the Woolfs had never been anywhere near Virginia.

Jerry suddenly burst into life. 'Okay, now I get it! You know, you Limeys are the worst. You look like you couldn't snuff a candle, but you sure know how to *blow!*' Oliver sensed his cheeks redden. 'And boy, Bruce can blow the whole house. Know what I mean?

Practically have 'em lined up round the block!' Jerry took a red handkerchief from his back pocket and mopped his brow.

'Bruce is a bit poorly right now', said Oliver. 'You might find he's lost some of his old vigour.'

'Sorry to hear that. Nothin' serious, I hope. We've lost some good friends this past year. Damn virus is goin' through this city like a scythe.'

'Why don't you ask me about Candy?' said the girl at the bar, when Jerry had gone. 'I couldn't help overhearing.'

'Oliver, this is Jackie T', said Irina.

Jackie T looked and sounded exactly like Jackie O, circa 1960. She had the smooth helmet of hair, the doe eyes, the East Hampton purr, and the Perfect Pink lipstick. But size ten feet and an Adam's apple. The black rubber gown and opera gloves were doubtless another departure from the original. Oliver looked for the telltale bulge beneath the latex, but there wasn't one.

Irina winked: 'Excuse me, hon, I have to powder my nose, but you're in good hands.' She turned away: another set-up.

'You know Candy?' he asked.

'Sure ... Candy Fredricks.'

So that was it, another piece of the jigsaw.

'You know, you're the only person I've heard use her last name. Sounds like you're good friends.'

'We were kinda close. Like Jerry said, she used to come here a lot. And we've all tried out stuff together.'

'You didn't see her here in the summer?'

'No, I was out of town.'

'Oh, that's a pity. So, is this where you met?'

'Not the first time. I ran into her one night at a dance club. She was pogoing her butt off, and so was I, and we ended up together in a heap on the floor. She was wearing a black bin-liner dress — sort of *homage à* Debbie Harry. Had her hair cut the same way too. She was kinda cool.'

'What was she doing in New York ... were her parents living here?'

'Are you crazy? She was a runaway. A wild child. She was squatting in some place in Alphabet City with a creep she hooked up with in a tattoo parlour ... the guy Jerry mentioned.'

'Did he come here too?'

'Off and on. But they used to hang out in other places, like Anvil, which were way too left field for me.'

'Anvil — what sort of place is that?'

'Hardcore. Your friend Bruce used to go. Probably still does, for all I know. You should ask him about it. It's strictly men only, but Candy used to drag up. She can make a convincing boy when she wants. Should've been a dyke. The girl can be a real hardnosed bitch too. A solid gold heart breaker. You wanna be careful.'

'Thanks, I'll watch out.' Jackie offered a cigarette, but he declined. 'And you, did you grow up here?'

'In Manhattan you mean? No, I'm a New Jersey girl! I used to come up on the train. They call it the "Dinky". It only has a couple of cars and there's no bathroom, so I'd change where I sat. I was a preppy teenager by day and a Punk princess by night. I got a kick out of reinventing myself on the move.'

'I'd like to have seen that.'

'You're not the only one. I used to have quite an audience.' She fixed him with a Jackie-O, laser look. 'Y'know, you're kinda cute for an English boy. Why don't you stay a while, buy Jackie a drink?'

26

Tottenham Court Road lay silent and unswept, animated only by a solitary bus heading north. The pavement was broken and uneven, the litter bins overflowed. Even the electrical-goods shops had rolled down their shutters, closed to the bargain hunters on Sundays. It would be hard to imagine a less promising residential address. Candy rang Luke's doorbell.

He buzzed her in. The front door was of a riot-proof pattern, a dull silver rectangle cut into the red faience wall of Goodge Street station. From the outside there was no hint of habitation. The door might have opened on to a service shaft or an electrical substation, and the narrow hallway gave no further clues. Decorated in shades of railway brown, it smelt musty and abandoned; junk mail spread like a fungus across the floor. The landlord had bought out most of the tenants, but Luke was a refusenik. Candy shook the rain from her umbrella and pressed the button for the rickety lift.

Luke's flat was on the sixth floor. He called it the 'penthouse', but its sole distinction was access to the roof, where you could sunbathe naked without being overlooked.

Luke was waiting for her on the landing. 'So, now I have you in *my* web', he said. Candy didn't respond, just followed him into the sitting room. Furnished in accents of leather and chrome — a fetishist's home décor — it was cold in every sense, the ancient radiator making no pretence at warmth.

'I like the splash of colour', he said, stroking her leather skirt. 'Red suits you. You should wear it more often. Now take everything off … slowly!' Silently, she unbuttoned her sweater and slipped it over her head, then unzipped the skirt and let it tumble to the floor. 'Wait … I want to look at you.' She had her hand on her bra strap, ready to release the clasp, and paused as instructed.

'Go on …' She straightened her back, emphasising the firmness of her breasts, then reached down and unzipped her ankle boots, stepping out of them in turn. 'Stop … that's enough for now.'

She stood in her G-string and stockings, aroused but apprehensive, goose bumps forming, not knowing what he had in store for her.

The hardest part of her relationship with Luke had been reaching the point where she could relinquish control. But what is a lifelong dom to do when she discovers that she needs someone emotionally and physically, and that someone happens to be a dominant-submissive switch with a mind as magnificently inventive as her own? Who shall dominate the dominatrix?

The only solution was an accommodation of some kind. It had been Luke's idea, but she'd acquiesced, partly because she trusted him, but mostly to satisfy an inexpressible need. She had to be with him, to lie beside him, to breathe in the warm air next to his skin. Thus, they entered a reciprocal world of pleasure and pain. She was free to inflict whatever indignity she wished upon him, provided he was allowed to repeat it on her, and vice versa. It was a system that imposed restraint yet invited exploration. It also worked in strict rotation. Today was his turn. That was the other part of the bargain: the top always commanded his or her own territory.

'Sit down', Luke continued: 'Relax. And spread yourself out so that I can tie you properly.' He opened a black Gladstone bag and took out a roll of vinyl tape. First, he secured her wrists, then her ankles, winding the tape in a figure of eight around the chair's tubular frame, tight enough to hold her, but not enough to hurt. 'Now we're going to put this on', he said. It was a blindfold, of the kind they give you on an aircraft, but made from soft black neoprene. He eased it over her eyes.

'What else do you keep in your handbag?' she asked, her nose finally getting the better of her.

'Just a spare pair of underpants', he said. 'My mother taught me always to be prepared.'

She sniggered and heard him leave the room, the soles of his leather moccasins squeaking against the polished wooden floor.

Sounds began to emanate from the kitchen, as if he were preparing a meal. How long was he going to keep her waiting? The technique was familiar: the path to submission begins with suspense, not suffering. He was punishing her for stepping out of role. She should have known better than to laugh. He might leave her there for hours. Drifting into sleep would be a second act of rebellion.

Finally, approaching footsteps signalled his return. He placed something heavy on the floor. A metallic click and the clatter of a cassette tape told her what it was. A brief silence then the rising cadences of the music. Sonorous and magnificent, it soared and sparkled: it electrified the air. She closed her eyes and the transcendent sound world enveloped her; it was soothing, dreamy, narcotic.

A freezing sensation on her lips jolted her awake. She licked it. Mmm, a ball of ice, perfectly smooth and round. He held the ball against her tongue, until she feared she'd lose all feeling, then began to trace a path around her chin and down her neck, descending slowly towards her breasts, over her belly, and beneath the silky gauze of her G-string. He worked her with his finger, gently, rhythmically, then ... 'YOW!' He tucked the ice right up inside her. She clamped involuntarily. Fuck, it was cold! The coldest cunt in Christendom.

'Was that good?'

'No, are you kidding?'

'Then let's try something different ...' She caught the heat of a flame and the scent of candle wax. 'This evening's adventure is a play of contrasts: hot and cold, wet and dry, rough and smooth. And we have *Parsifal* to accompany us for the next four hours.'

A cool trickle of meltwater soaked into her pants, and she had an irresistible urge to pee. Pregnancy seemed to have shrunk her bladder to half its former size. You want wet, well here it is. And anyway, what's a little puddle between friends?

27

Oliver dropped his bags and pressed the button on the answering machine. There was a message from the *Telegraph*. 'Darling, it's Marjorie. Not sure if you're back, but could you possibly let me have your Philip Johnson piece today. We have a gap to fill. Thank you so much.'

He loved M. She was elegant and unflappable, the *Telegraph*'s Honor Blackman, but even so. 'Bugger!' He pushed the button again and heard Nola: 'Ollie ... you'll never guess what? I flew back on *Concorde*! Give me a call.'

How did she wangle that? There couldn't be a greater contrast with his own miserable flight in steerage on Pan Am, stuck beside two hags from the Bronx, or some other hellhole. They'd yakked all night, even imitated his accent — 'did'ya hear, he said *wartah*!' — talking as if he weren't there.

He phoned Nola and got her machine. Then he tried Candy's number, but it just rang. No surprise on either count. He flicked through his mail. Nothing interesting: a bank statement, a handful of bills and junk from American Express, tormenting him with the prospect of a gold card. He tossed it all on the table unopened and turned his attention to the coffee percolator.

By four o'clock he'd finished the piece and was ready to hand it in. It was good. Perhaps not as sharp as it might have been given another few hours, but he was pleased with it, nonetheless. Johnson wouldn't be, he was certain. But then if you can't upset someone like Philip Johnson what's the point of being a critic? He fed the four pages into the fax machine and called to make sure they'd gone through.

'Yes. Thank you, Oliver darling. All safe and sound. I knew you'd come up trumps.'

'My pleasure Moneypenny.' Why couldn't all women be like M? He replaced the receiver and Nola called almost immediately.

'The flight was fabulous', she said: 'Three-and-a-half hours instead of eight. Have you ever done it?'

'I'm afraid not. It's way out of my income bracket. You're very lucky.'

'Not lucky, well connected. A friend of mine's a British Airways pilot. I gave him my dates and he wangled me an upgrade on the way back.'

'How was it?'

'It's a bit like being in a Ferrari with a hundred seats and an endless supply of bubbly. And guess who I sat next to?'

'The only person I know who flies supersonic is David Frost.'

'Puh-leeze ...'

'Okay, I give up.'

'Claudette Colbert!'

'Wow, I didn't know she was still alive. She must be at least a hundred.'

'Eighty-one ... she told me. She has an apartment in Manhattan but spends most of the year in Barbados. I asked her how she managed to stay so fit, and she said, "sex and sunshine darling". She's adorable. Exactly how I hope I'll be when I'm too old to bend over!'

'You seem to have a weakness for geriatric movie stars.'

'It's true, I do. But stupidly, I didn't ask for an autograph.'

'So, how does it feel to fly that fast?'

'It's hard to say. There's nothing outside to gauge your speed by, no clouds or anything. When we hit Mach 2 the captain made a little announcement. He was a darling. You know there have been more US astronauts than there are Concorde pilots. Even if you laid all the pilots end-to-end, you could still be home in time for tea.'

It was the longest telephone conversation he'd had with her. He wasn't sure whether it was a good sign or not.

'Are you still looking for your friend?' she asked, just as he assumed she was going say goodbye.

He'd drafted a note to Candy, which had been lying next to his typewriter while he'd been away. Problem was he had no idea how to get it to her. He explained his dilemma.

'Well, if your hunch about the mews is right, why don't you put the same note through every letterbox?' she said. 'One of them is bound to reach her.' It was such a brilliant idea; he didn't mind that she'd made him look like an idiot again.

A visit to the newsagent, and he had fifty photocopies and a pack of envelopes. He addressed each one *Candy Fredricks — Private by Hand* and put them in his satchel. Ten minutes later he was in the mews. He'd posted five letters and had the next one ready, when from the corner of his eye he saw the taillights of a white Mercedes roadster disappearing round the corner. It looked like the car he'd seen parked there before.

28

'Catherine darling ... this came for you. They must have put it through my letterbox by mistake.' Candy looked at the envelope and turned it over. How very odd — that made two. She'd found the first letter on the mat when she got back, and now here was its twin. 'Thank you, Mrs Abrams', she said, but the old lady had already closed her door. She slipped the letter in her pocket and headed for the Underground. George had summoned her, and she didn't want to be late.

The pub George had chosen was gloomy and unexceptional, template Victoriana. It suited him perfectly. Candy forced her way through the early evening drinkers to a nook at the far end of the bar, where George was sitting. 'Sorry if I'm late', she said. 'The Tube's all over the place. Person under a train or something.'

'No problem. I should apologise for dragging you all the way over here.' He tapped his pipe out in the ashtray. 'It's not much of a place, I'm afraid, but the boys at the Yard like it. Coppers are like burglars; they don't like to stray too far from home.' He waited for her to respond, but she blanked him. He frowned and upped the pomposity setting a notch. 'I've asked a chap from Forensics to join us, but before he gets here, I'd like to fill you in on progress.'

'Good, I was beginning to think you'd forgotten about me.'

'Don't be like that. You know I need to be careful. Now, first things first: let me get you a drink. What'll it be?'

'I'll have a vodka and tonic … thanks.'

'Well then, the story so far', George began. 'The big news is that they think they've identified Diessel. His dabs were all over your place.' Her heart leaped then settled into a staccato beat. 'They found mine too, which was a bit embarrassing. Should have thought about that before I helped you.'

'Where is he now?'

'Don't worry, nowhere you're ever likely to go. He's based down in Croydon. Crosses the river for recreation. You know, doesn't like to dirty his own doorstep. They traced him about a week ago. His real name's Pedersen. Maybe Danish originally, though he's been here for years.'

'Another fucking Viking. How did they track him down?'

'One of the lads had a hunch that Diessel might be an alias he'd used before, so we asked around and hey presto, it's his moniker in some of the nastier clubs. Turns out he's got form and the local plod have been keeping tabs on him, so the rest was easy. Next step is to get a positive ID. They'll arrange a line-up when they bring him in. Think you'll be able to handle that?'

'I don't know. I only saw his face in the light for about thirty seconds. But it's definitely him on the tape.'

'Perhaps this will help?' George produced a black-and-white police mug shot and laid it on the table. 'It was taken two years ago, but he can't have changed much since then.'

'I think it's him. Except he's not wearing glasses, so I couldn't swear to it. What else have you got on him?'

'This and that.'

'Really George, it's like getting blood from a stone!' Withholding evidence was a way of life for some people.

'All right, no need to get on your high horse! He started out in the Sixties as a croupier, working at the Clermont Club. Got a reputation as a bit of a smooth operator and ended up as manager of another club, called the Berkeley, but they got shut down about the same time as the Clermont.'

'I'll ask Olga if she's come across him. She used to mix with the Clermont set. Is that it?'

'He's about my age …'

'Don't be ridiculous George, nobody's *that* old!'

'… and apparently, he likes to be tied up. By men or women, doesn't seem too fussy. Could be significant.'

'You said he's got form … what sort of form?'

'He was up on a rape charge two years ago, just before the Berkeley closed. Hence the mug shot. He managed to get off though. Someone put the frighteners on the girl, and she refused to testify. Draw your own conclusions.'

'So, what's he doing in Croydon?'

'Seems he's slipped a few rungs down the social ladder since the rape case. The Mayfair crowd gave him the cold shoulder. Runs a club down there called The Big O. It's basically a teenage flesh market. Jimmy Savile does a gig once a month. Gets paid in kind apparently, the younger the better.'

'Ugh! I wouldn't let Jim fix anything for me.'

'He has another little sideline too. Knows how to hustle the muscle. Supplies bouncers for nightclubs, that kind of thing. A pretty iffy business by all accounts. And he still likes to deal a bit, only now it's drugs and girls. Your standard toerag to riches story, basically.'

'Sounds delightful. What about Margrét?'

'No sign, sorry. She left the house the night we made the recording and hasn't been seen since. My man didn't spot anyone else leaving, so Pedersen most likely left through the garden at the back. Anyway, they can't find him either. He's gone to ground.'

'Are you sure they're really looking?'

'Well, we haven't alerted Interpol', he said, 'or closed the borders, but so far as anyone can tell they've both disappeared.'

Really, she could do without his sarcasm. 'Do you have any idea how the two of them met?'

'No, but as I said, he goes to some iffy clubs. There's a couple of Berliners who have a scene going in a warehouse down Wapping way. Place called Gore. She could have hooked up with him there, I guess.'

George finished his beer and wiped his mouth with the back of his hand. 'Oh, and there's something else', he said, as if it were incidental. 'You might like to know they identified the girl in the morgue. She's called Mary McCartney. From Dublin originally. She was working the streets round your way. Lived in a squat behind the station with a dozen other girls. One of them eventually reported her missing.'

'How did she die; did they tell you?'

'She was a heroin addict. And she'd been primed with alcohol. But that's not what killed her. She had a cardiac arrest. Could've dropped dead on the spot or fallen into a coma and died of hypothermia. They can't be sure. At any rate, she'd been dead a couple of hours when they brought her in.'

'So, case closed then?'

'Not necessarily. They found traces of chloroform in her blood. That might be an alternative scenario for heart failure. If they pursue that line, we're possibly looking at a murder inquiry.'

George stood up: 'Candy, this is Cyril Armitage from Forensics.' Cyril could have been Laurel to George's Hardy. He held out a limp hand and said hello. His breath smelt of extra-strong mints, a telltale of the career alcoholic.

'The prof's been working on our case. He's going to tell us what they found in your rooms. Prof why don't you bring Candy up to speed while I get the drinks in?' Cyril puffed up and cleared his throat. She added self-importance to his growing list of charms.

'Well, we studied the blood spots you found using something called bloodstain pattern analysis. It's a simple technique that tells us the direction in which the blood spatter travelled and the angle at which it struck the surface — in this case the carpet. I'll spare you the mathematics, suffice to say that if we triangulate, it allows us to determine the area of origin.'

'And what did that tell you?'

'In fact, we discovered something rather interesting. The spatters are formed into distinct groups. At least four or five, possibly more. It's difficult to be precise because the groups are overlaid to some degree. However, the angle of impact within these groups is consistent: mainly perpendicular. In other words, the droplets fell as drips. These groups correspond with use of the harness and the blood residue we found there. That could indicate restraint during the trauma, or that the victim was sedated and incapable of movement.'

She shuddered at the memory of the cold chloroform. 'You said four or five: you mean there was more than one victim?'

'Quite possibly, yes. We found something else that could be material. All the samples are from females, which one might have assumed, but analysis revealed three different groups: O-negative and positive, and B-negative. Group O is commonplace here, so you would expect a preponderance. But B-negative is very rare indeed. Only about two per cent of us are B-negative ... including the girl in the morgue.'

'You think she was one of the victims?'

'I can't say with absolute certainty, but it's likely, yes.'

'Do you have any idea when all this started?'

'It's hard to say. Our luminol test showed up some quite old blood residue, which you couldn't have seen with the naked eye. Dried blood tends to lose coloration over time, and the carpet doesn't help. Overall, I'd say all the samples are dateable to within the past two or three months, with the most recent stains no more than a few days old when we found them.'

Two months placed the first incident in mid-September. So, it was possible they'd begun using her rooms shortly after she was attacked. But he was suggesting they'd been using them even before that. Another reason for Margrét to want her out of the way. Means, motive, and opportunity. They had all three.

George returned with the drinks: 'Cheers everyone! Here's to a life of crime.' Cyril looked up, irritated.

'Now I'm afraid I've told you rather more than I should. I trust none of this will go any further?'

'Absolutely', said George. 'You have my word.'

'Sure', said Candy, 'who would I tell anyway?'

29

Nola lit a cigarette and inhaled deeply. 'That's your third', he said. 'And anyway, you know you're not supposed to smoke in the galleries.'

'I'm sorry — I didn't know you were counting.'

'Look, don't get upset. I mean it's not good for you, that's all.'

'Do you want me to put it out?'

'Not if you're enjoying it. But I do want you to look after yourself.'

'I'm touched', she said, obviously annoyed.

Since he'd begun seeing her, it was only the fourth time they'd managed to spend a day together. The last thing he wanted to do was to spoil it by sparking an argument, but he didn't seem able to change the mood.

They'd come to the Royal Academy to see the Thyssen-Bornemisza collection: her idea not his. Inspired by a New York period Dalí, Nola had picked up the threads of a conversation about Dalí and Gala, embarked upon in the St Regis, and begun to decode Dalí's elaborate dreamscape. She was dazzled by it, but he couldn't work up much enthusiasm. He was more interested in the fact that Dalí's levitating nude, with her tiny waist and gymnast's thighs, could have been Liza's body double, but he suppressed that observation.

She was in full-on Courtauld mode, the keenest kid in the class, the top Marks: '... you have to remind yourself that Dalí is a Catholic. In Christian allegory the Virgin Mary is sometimes represented by a queen bee, so the fact that the female figure is about to be stung — impregnated — might also suggest the Immaculate Conception. But the significance of the pomegranate is more complex. In devotional art it represents resurrection and everlasting life. Yet it's also an ancient fertility symbol. You know the myth of Persephone?'

'Remind me ...'

'Persephone is the daughter of Demeter and Zeus. Hades abducts her and carries her into the Underworld to be his bride. Zeus forces Hades to let her go. But there's a catch. The Fates rule that anyone who takes nourishment in the Underworld must remain there. Hades tricks Persephone into eating pomegranate seeds. It means she must return to him for four months of the year.'

'And her release heralds the coming of spring. But it's not a mythological piece, right?'

'No, there's another twist. Persephone is a chthonic deity — *dread* Persephone, queen, and guide of the Underworld. Jungians use the term *chthonic* to describe the unconscious, earthly impulses of the self: things like envy, lust, sensuality, and perversion. The water offers another clue. It represents the Styx — the river that winds around Hades — and a journey to the other side.'

'Bruce says a journey is a fragment of hell.'

'In this case it's a journey of sexual discovery, of sexual awakening. I suppose that might be hell if you're not sure which direction to follow, or how far you want to go.'

She sounded uncannily like Alice; not a conversation he wanted to pursue. 'So how do you know so much about this piece?' he asked, by way of diversion.

'It's one of the paintings I studied for my thesis.'

'Tell me about it, I'm intrigued.'

'My thesis? I called it *The Cultural Libido*, but they pretended not to know what that meant, so they made me add a subtitle: *How Sexuality Motivates Art*. I argued that that the sexual drive and creative drive are two ways of expressing the same primal force.'

'You're talking about sublimation?'

'Exactly. When we talk about erotic art, we really mean that art on to which we can most easily project our own lusts and desires. I began with Durer's *The Fall of Man* and ended with Kubrick's *Clockwork Orange*.'

'Why *Clockwork Orange*?'

'Mostly for the rape scene. Its violence is at the opposite end of the spectrum from *The Fall*, which is essentially idyllic. And I wanted to include Allen Jones' rubber waitresses for the Korova Milk Bar. They're *very* kinky.'

'I've seen the film, but I don't remember them.'

'No, you wouldn't. They didn't make it into the movie. Kubrick refused to pay Allen for the commission. He's such a dick. I have one of the outfits, though. I wear it on special occasions. If you buck up, I'll show you one day …'

He'd just got home when she phoned. 'Ollie, I'm sorry I was such a grump earlier', she said. 'Let's try again. Let's pretend it's our anniversary and go for dinner. I'll book us a room. We can talk and make plans. It will be fun.'

'Okay, where do you suggest?' He didn't even pretend to resist.

'Meet me in the American Bar, tomorrow at seven.'

'How will I recognise you?' he said, hoping to make her laugh.

'I'll wear my heart on my sleeve, so you can't miss it.'

* * *

The sound of Hoagy Carmichael's *The Nearness of You* being tortured on the piano drifted through the lobby. In its glory days, one might have found Dinah Shore singing here, or Frank Sinatra, or Dean Martin. The Savoy had a good line in boozers and crooners.

Oliver knew the American Bar as a place of careworn opulence. An Art Deco curiosity, never a masterpiece, it grew more atmospheric after dark. It must have been much the same on the old Cunarders, crossing the Atlantic. Out of time, and out of style, but ploughing on.

161

There she was, dressed in a grey woollen suit, looking demure. Only her heels offered any encouragement. He pecked her cautiously on the cheek and sat down beside her.

'What are you drinking?'

'A White Lady. It's the house speciality — Gordon's, Cointreau, lemon juice — probably not your thing. Let's ask Vic what he recommends.'

Vic was the head barman, a Savoy institution. He studied Oliver carefully, as if he were an anthropological specimen. 'I think an Old Fashioned would suit you, sir. It has a whisky base.' Savoy barmen were a higher life form, he decided, with supernatural powers of intuition.

The ancient wood panelling creaked and groaned as the lift made its stately progress to the sixth floor. When they reached the room, it was disappointingly bland: a symphony in beige, with over-sized sale-room furniture and a faded Persian carpet. Not what he had expected at all. The residual scent of cigarettes and other people's sex had an immediate detumescent effect.

'Whistler slept here', Nola said, perching on the end of the bed. 'At least that's what they tell you.'

'When was that?'

'Some time in the late eighteen-nineties. His wife was dying and so they came back from Paris. I don't think he trusted Froggy doctors. He made a series of drawings from that balcony. They must have stayed here for quite a while.'

He peered through the rain-streaked window. All he could make out were the lights of the traffic moving sluggishly on Waterloo Bridge and the grey monolith of the National Theatre. It would be hard to imagine anyone romanticising such a scene. 'I don't think I've ever seen them.'

'There's a drawing of his wife that's particularly touching. She's lying on a day bed in front of the window, wrapped up against the cold. It's very tender ... quite uncharacteristic.'

He closed the curtains and pulled back the covers on the bed. 'I really care about you, you know', he said. 'I'd like to try to make

162

a go of it if you're serious.' He stroked her arm, and she pulled him close: 'Come here silly boy, I mean to make amends ...'

He was thrown out politely just after twelve. Ordinarily he'd have been offended, but for once he was almost grateful. The whole experience had been strangely depressing. There was no warmth, no urgency, no sense of desire. Nola might have delegated her role to someone else. The suspicion that someone had been there before him was reinforced.

He'd registered every tiny imperfection. The fading bruises on her neck, the stubble under her arms, a smudge of lipstick on her teeth. Even the room had irked: a burn mark on the carpet, a fraying edge to the sheet.

His fault-finding mission had begun over dinner in the Grill. The slowness of the service, and the lukewarm sirloin from the trolley, had irritated. The way she'd scanned the room as he was talking, and the furtive smile she'd exchanged with their neighbour, had infuriated.

At some point he'd simply stopped believing in her. Or more precisely he'd resumed his disbelief. Her gravitational pull was weakening.

December 1984

30

Alone in the stairwell, Candy felt her stomach loop the loop. Why she should be so wary of Alice, she wasn't sure. That's just the way it was. Alice was from another world, a parallel dimension, with supernatural powers, sixth and seventh senses. She would get inside your head and articulate your thoughts before you'd even formed them. And once she was in, there was no getting her out. Alice was able to guide you as if you were on rails. But it was time to talk. The key was in its usual place under the mat, so she unlocked the door.

Alice was at the kitchen counter, filling a kettle. She stared in mock alarm, as if she'd confronted an apparition. 'Oh my!' she said, 'The prodigal returns. Where have you been all this time, honey? I missed you.'

'I've been hiding', she said. 'Something happened.' Alice hugged her tight and kissed her on both cheeks. 'Now sit down and tell me everything ... I'm just making coffee.'

For a moment, in the permanent half-light of the studio, she didn't see the figure lounging on the bed. And then she couldn't quite believe it was possible, the depth of betrayal it signified was too great. There, wrapped in Alice's silk dressing gown, casually smoking a cigarillo, was Margrét. 'Excuse me, but what the *Holy Fuck* is she doing here?'

'She's my friend ... our friend', said Alice. 'She's got into a fight and needs my help. So, she's staying here for a while.'

'You must be joking! Has she told you what she and her creepy sidekick did to me?'

'Margrét has explained everything, right from the beginning. And I have to say I'm disappointed I had to hear about it from her and not you. I thought we had an understanding. But you're a big girl now. You oughta be able to look after yourself.' Which was true in a way. If she'd followed her own rules, she would never have gone up to Diessel's room. But she'd been sloppy and suffered the consequences. 'She's just a kid. And she's as much a victim as you are.'

'How long has she been here?'

'Since she was attacked. She needed somewhere safe to stay and so I took her in.'

Candy glared at Margrét: 'So what happened?'

'He cut me up!'

'Who?'

'Pedersen, of course. Who d'you think?' She opened her dressing gown to reveal a finely woven pattern of cuts to her abdomen. He'd excelled himself.

'It was you, screaming Rosebud, wasn't it?'

'How do you know that?'

'You were caught on tape. Quite a performance.' Margrét smirked knowingly at Alice, but the look was not returned. 'You watched him slice all the others, but reckoned it could never happen to you ... right? Well, what goes around comes around!'

'Now you two, stop fighting!' said Alice. The dog Severin growled in his basket, as if ready to do his mistress's bidding.

'Candy I'm sorry for what I did ... truly!' said Margrét. She began to cry, big drippy crocodile tears. Alice gave her a tissue and she paused theatrically to blow her nose. 'I didn't know he was going to hurt you. Honestly! I wanted to give you a surprise, that's all!'

'Liar! Did she tell you what she's been up to with her psycho boyfriend? They've been running a night shift in my rooms and carving up girls for fuck knows how long. That's why she set me up — to scare me away!'

'Candy you're becoming hysterical', said Alice. 'Margrét made a wrong call, that's all. She's said she's sorry. Why can't we leave it at that?'

'Because I could have died, that's why. Like Mary McCartney! I suppose you only wanted to scare her too?'

'Mary's dead? Oh, please God no ...' Margrét began her crocodile routine again, sobbing loudly this time.

'Yes, I saw her laid out on a gurney. Count yourself lucky you're not lying there beside her.'

Margrét now looked genuinely distraught, her face a molten mess of snot and tears, but Candy was damned if she was going to feel sorry for her. The cunning little bitch could jump in the river for all she cared. It was interesting, though, how completely she'd managed to seduce Alice. She must have played on her weakness for young flesh.

'Is she going to report this?' Candy asked Alice. 'We can add it to the charge sheet. He'll definitely go down if we both testify.'

'No please … I'm scared!' wailed Margrét: 'I can't face him in court! I never want to see him again!'

'I don't exactly relish the prospect either, but we've got to stop him somehow, even if it means chopping all his fucking fingers off. Where's he hiding?'

The crying ceased as abruptly as it had started. 'I've no idea', she said, 'and even if I knew I wouldn't tell you. If he finds out I've told you anything he'll kill me!'

'Now stop it you two', said Alice. 'You can forget about the police. They're never going to pin anything on him if nobody's willing to testify. And none of us wants to be dragged through the courts. We'll have to find a way of dealing with him in our own way.'

Candy phoned George as soon as she got home. 'Well, well', he said, 'so much for loyalty and friendship. You realise I'll have to go to the police with this. They'll want to bring her in. She's an accessory, don't forget.'

'Can't we buy some time? Wait and see if Alice's scheme will work? I don't see much point in going after Margrét if she's not going to help convict him.' Alice's plan was elegant, but whether it would work or not was anyone's guess.

'Look, I'm sympathetic. But what you're proposing is basically a vigilante operation. And I can't afford to get mixed up in something like that.'

'You don't have to get involved. Just pretend this conversation never happened, that's all. Then keep quiet until the party's over. Please George, I'm not asking much. Just do it for me!'

31

Halfway down the mews, Oliver heard the music. It grew louder as he progressed. It dawned on him what it was: Nico's plangent rendition of Lou Reed's *Femme Fatale*.

He waited beneath the open window and listened to the end. It must be her. But what would he do if he was wrong? Pretend he was a Mormon? No, they always came in pairs. Say he was canvassing for the Conservatives? That ought to get the door slammed in his face. He rang the bell. No answer. He rang again and a shock of pink hair shot out of the window above. 'Candy?'

'Oliver! How on earth did you find me here?'

'I turned detective. Can I come in?'

'Just a second … I'll come down.'

'I've been worried about you … are you all right?' he asked when she opened the door.

'I'm sorry', she said. 'I'm fine. My life's a bit upside down at the moment, that's all.'

'I left you a note … did you get it?'

'Uh-huh, two in fact. I was wondering whether to call you.'

'You know you're a very difficult person to find.'

'Good', she said: 'That's how I like it.'

'So why did you vanish like that?'

'I had an epiphany.'

'Do you want to tell me about it?'

'Not right now, no. I'm sorry … I didn't mean to be rude.'

'Look, I understand … at least I'm trying to. But promise me you won't disappear again.'

'Enough! Come upstairs. Careful, they're a bit steep.'

She set the track to play from the beginning again. The album sleeve was on the coffee table, and he picked it up.

'It's the first record I bought', she said. 'It always cheers me up. Five minutes ago, you'd have caught me with *I'm Waiting for the Man.*' Her face conceded a smile.

He laughed, relieved that the tension had been broken. Glancing around the room he spotted one of Alice's photo collages leaning against the wall. In the foreground were three voluptuous women whose figures had been cropped tightly to conceal heads and feet. Behind was Alice's own slender body, partially hidden from view.

'I've seen Alice's exhibition', he said: 'But I don't recall this one.'
'She didn't show it. It's from a very limited edition.' Candy seemed preoccupied. 'So, tell me Mr Detective, how do you know Alice?'
'I went to Maitresse …'
'Really?' she said, in obvious amazement. 'You *have* been busy. I can't believe you've even heard of it?'
'A friend mentioned it. I had a hunch I'd find you there.'
'Ordinarily you would, but I haven't been out for weeks. I've been holed up here for so long I'm starting to feel like Rapunzel.'
'Hence the hair …'
'Uh-huh, I had it done a couple of weeks ago. I needed to lighten the mood. Keith at Smile did it for me.'
'Am I supposed to know who he is?'
'He does Toyah's hair. If you ever feel like changing colour or having a Mohican, he's the guy to go to.'
'Oh, I see. Thanks, I'll keep it in mind. I don't think I've ever seen you in colours before, but you wear them well.'
'Thanks … it's the beginning of my un-black period.'
She was wearing purple leggings and a green skirt, with a baggy woollen top whose colour was somewhere between crimson and magenta. Add the coral hair and the effect was quite painterly.
'So, what did you make of Maitresse?' she asked, more like her old self. 'I'm beginning to think you're a very dark horse.'
'Well, first of all I was surprised they let me in. I didn't have anything suitable in my wardrobe, only my old leather jacket and black jeans.'
'Okay, borderline rejection. Who was on the door?'
'A terrifying girl who looked like she'd stepped out of *Blade Runner*.'
'Sounds like Lily. She's cool. She probably took a shine to you.'
'Actually, she said hello last time.'
'Oh, *I see* … so you've been more than once?'
'Only twice', he said defensively. 'How do you know her?'
'She used to help me in my rooms. You know about them too I suppose?'
'Alice mentioned them, but she was a bit vague. She gave me

what she said was a work number. I rang and left a message. Maybe you never got it. But she didn't say where your rooms were.'

'That's probably because she's never been there. They're not so far from you, actually. On the other side of the canal. You used to be on my way home. Olga, the woman who owns the house, lets me use the first floor. She's retired now, but she was *the* go-to madam in her heyday. She used to supply girls for the Cliveden pool parties. You know, Profumo and all that.'

'I know the basics ...'

'Olga and Stephen Ward were friends. I think they played the field together. She used to ferry the girls down there in her Jaguar, three or four at a time. It was a kinky crowd ...' she paused.

'Tell me', he said.

'I can't. I've already told you too much. If the real story got out Olga would have me hung. And don't think I'm joking.'

'You make it sound like the Mafia.'

'It's much worse than that. There are some very powerful people involved. Some of them would lose everything if the world discovered what they'd been doing after dark. And one or two have a *very* long way to fall.'

'So, weren't they taking an incredible risk?'

'I guess so, but that's life.' She paused again. 'What else did Alice tell you?'

'She said you were a pro-domme, not a tart.'

'Well now you know. It's not a huge secret, although I'm now officially an ex-domme. I'm resting and in no hurry to return. Anyway, enough of that. You haven't told me what you made of the club.'

'I suppose I was quite intimidated at first. I didn't know what to expect. In the end, though, I rather enjoyed it. They were a friendly bunch. Mostly anyway. I was struck by the sense of camaraderie.'

'That's an interesting observation. We pervs generally like to stick together.'

Curiously, even though he'd been better prepared, and sported his Hellfire T-shirt, he hadn't enjoyed his second visit to Maitresse nearly as much as he'd hoped. But then perhaps all second experiences were like that. Nothing can ever match the excitement you feel the first time.

He'd found Alice in one of the vaults, preparing for a *Kinbaku* masterclass. She'd invited him to join her, but he'd said, 'maybe next time'. Not because he didn't like the idea of being bound, he was just wary of yielding control. Once the balance tipped too far in her favour, he decided, it might not easily be regained. Although had Nola asked, he would have submitted willingly.

As the music stopped, the conversation stalled. Candy appeared distracted, more interested in leafing through her records than talking. While she browsed, he picked up Alice's photograph and examined it more carefully. The central figure faced the camera. The other two were turned at an angle, as if all three were about to embrace. He recognised the allusion; and something else: the girl on the right had a kidney-shaped mole on her inner thigh. 'That's Nola!' he exclaimed, sounding more surprised than he would have liked.

'Oh, so you know her too?' said Candy, looking over his shoulder.

'Yes, we've become quite close in the last few weeks.'

'Well, I'm glad you keep your eyes open. Who else can you see?'

'I don't know … Alice is in the background, but I've no idea who the other two are.'

'Hazard a guess.'

Examining the figure on the left more closely, he detected the edge of a tattoo beneath her arm: 'Is that you?'

'And the other one? You probably met her at the club …'

'Is that Liza in the middle?'

'*Very* good!'

He looked at the photograph with renewed interest.

'Now what else can you tell me?'

'Well, there's a story, obviously …' All three figures in the foreground had perfectly smooth skin. They looked waxy, though not cold: quite the opposite in fact. He paused, fixing on the torso of the newly discovered Liza.

'Go on …'

'None of you has any bodily hair.'

'That's Alice's doing. She has a complete phobia.'

'You mean she makes you shave it?'

'She's much more demanding that that. She insists on a whole depilatory routine. It's one of her ways of taking control. The first time I did it I felt weird afterwards, like a little girl again.'

'How often do you have to do it?'

'You really want to know? At least once a week. I quite enjoy it now though. It's become a kind of private ritual, almost meditative. She makes her boyfriends do it too. You should ask her about it.'

'Somehow I don't think Alice and I are ever going to be that close.'

'You never know …'

'She sounds like John Ruskin', he replied, trying to change the subject. 'He had a thing about pubic hair too.'

'You mean Ruskin the art critic? How interesting, I didn't know that.'

'Yes, before he was married, he had this idealised notion of the female body. I think he assumed that women were like Renaissance statuary, smooth and flawless. He couldn't reconcile himself to the reality between his wife's legs. He was horrified.'

'He would have got on very well with Alice then. But you haven't finished telling me what you can see in the photograph.'

'Well, you're goddesses, naturally. Perhaps the Three Graces — Charm, Beauty, and Creativity.'

'Alice calls us the Three Disgraces. It should have been the title of the photograph.'

'That's quite funny. But you're obviously more than models. There's a suggestion of intimacy …'

'Go on …'

He suddenly realised where the conversation was leading. It was obvious that Alice and Candy were close. And he should probably have guessed that Alice and Liza were too, but Alice and Nola? He had no idea they even knew one another. 'Are you all Alice's lovers?'

'Yes and no. Alice doesn't always feel the need to participate. She usually prefers to orchestrate. We were her novices. Still are in some ways; she's our guide.'

'I don't understand — novices in what sense?'

'She's a teacher, a kind of professor of sex. Her grandmother was a Korean comfort girl, so I think she sees it as some sort of cultural mission. She likes to help you find your sexual direction, to express your innermost desires. She calls it "integrating your shadow" if that means anything to you.' So that explained Alice's question. And the Jungian connection made sense too. The entire fetish scene was predicated on revealing one's hidden and rejected self, the transformation involved in dressing in rubber or leather being part of a liberating ritual. 'Alice can sort of read your mind. She's like a shaman.'

'Oh, I see. Can she read everyone so clearly?'

'She will have sensed *your* weaknesses, I'm sure.'

In retrospect, the strangest thing about the second evening at Maitresse was that when he told Alice he'd just returned from New York she'd just smiled and said, 'Congratulations! You're not the first person to have been liberated in Manhattan.'

Now he understood. She knew that his journey was already well advanced. She'd been plotting his trajectory vicariously through Nola, and via Nola through Irina and so on down the line. He imagined every juicy titbit being relayed on Alice's bush telegraph, her noting his progress and guiding the next move. He needn't have worried about resisting her advances, since he was already under her control. 'Did Alice know you were here, after you disappeared, I mean?' he asked

'I told no one.'

'You haven't been in touch with her?'

'Not until a few days ago, no. What's it to you, anyway?'

'I'm sorry, I didn't mean to pry. But you know I've been worried about you. I even dreamt about you.' He was beginning to sound pathetic.

'Given all the snooping you've been doing', said Candy, suddenly abrasive, 'you should know I'm never going to be your soft, cuddly girlfriend. I'm a dom, I'm mean, I'm cruel, I'm your worst frickin' nightmare. Do you understand?' He nodded, dumbly. 'In any case, even if Alice knew where I was, why would she tell you?

She's every right to be suspicious. We've learned to be wary of people we don't know turning up at our parties. They poke about, get you to reveal stuff about yourself and next thing it's splashed all over the *News of the World* or whatever. Someone gets labelled a pervert and they end up losing their job. They get hate mail. Their life falls apart. I've seen it happen.'

'But you know I'm not like that. I'm hardly even a real journalist. And anyway, I thought Alice liked me? We've spent quite a lot of time together.'

Candy's eyes softened. 'Look, I'm sure she does ... so do I. But that doesn't mean she's ready to *trust* you. It's different ... you must see that?'

It took a moment for the penny to drop. Alice wasn't the problem at all. Candy was projecting her own anxieties. 'Okay, let's stop there. Are you saying that *you're* not ready to trust me, is that it?'

'Maybe I am.'

'Well, that's fine. I won't ask any more questions. You just go at your own pace. And if you don't want me to come and see you, just say so. I'll be hurt, but I won't bother you again.'

The phone rang and Candy picked it up. 'Luke! Hello ... yes, me too. Look, I'm with someone just now. Can I call you back in five minutes?'

Saved by the bell: 'I'd better be going actually.'

'Sorry, just some business I have to sort out', she said, her hand over the receiver. 'Can you find your way out?'

'Sure. By the way, I nearly forgot ... Jackie T sends her love.' Candy froze, her face a study in horror and amazement. But before she could respond, he had made his escape. First rule of relationships: know when to leave.

Walking home, he ran through all the things he should have asked her and hadn't, such as: what was she doing for money; why had she put her life on hold; and why was she so insensitive to the needs of others? If he'd been a true friend, which he patently wasn't, he'd have got to the heart of the matter.

32

The discovery of Liza's naked form among Alice's Three Disgraces had provoked a desire of such intensity that Oliver simply had to see her. He had no idea what he was going to say, or what his next steps would be.

He waited a few seconds, straightened his tie, and rang the bell a second time. Finally, he heard approaching footsteps, and the door swung open. Liza was dressed down, in shiny rubber leggings and a pink New York Yankees sweatshirt. She didn't seem surprised to see him, or particularly impressed. 'I had a hunch it was you', she said, 'come on in.'

The smell of adhesive reached him before he got to the workroom. Set out on the big table were long pieces of white rubber, awaiting assembly. Stupid, he should have phoned. 'I'm sorry, I can see you're busy. Maybe I should come back another time?'

'No, don't be silly, I can always spare half an hour. If you don't mind waiting, I just want to seal this seam before the glue sets, and then we can go out.'

'What are you making?'

'It's a dress for Alice.'

He'd wondered how to broach the Alice question. 'A wedding dress?' he asked, hopefully.

'Ha ha ... I don't think that's very likely, do you? No, Alice is hosting a ball ... this is going to be her gown.'

'A pity. Alice seems to figure in my life rather a lot at the moment. I feel as if she's trying to take control. Have you ever felt like that?'

'About Alice? No, she's more of a mentor. She likes to help you find your true direction, to release your inner self.'

'Dalí's dream', he said.

She looked at him blankly.

'Sorry, I was thinking aloud. I saw a painting by Salvador Dalí a couple of days ago ... a dreamscape. What you've just said about Alice reminded me of it.'

'Oh ... I see.'

'But then when she's set you on your new path what does she do?'

175

'She likes to act as a sort of guardian angel. And to photograph you, of course — to record your progress. She's quite protective.'

'Protective or jealous?'

'Mostly protective ...'

'I thought you'd say that. But has she ever tried to stop you doing something?'

'Such as?'

'Such as sleeping with somebody?'

'No, never. At least not yet ...'

The conversation continued in the coffee shop, but Liza was fidgety, obviously keen to return to work. Perhaps it didn't matter. Half an hour in her company had been enough to prove his first impressions wrong. The plain Northern lass routine was simply a feint. She was quite the sophisticate, our Liza, if you cared to dig deeper, which he most certainly did. Easily the most talented of Alice's circle, she was far more attuned to his world than the others, more so even than Alice. And she possessed genuine warmth, which was rare indeed.

Fashion was hardly his remit, but her work was clearly special: a clever fusion of high-art and subcultural influences. An underground New Look. Whether the world was ready for rubber was anyone's guess. Probably not. But she could probably make it in the mainstream if she chose to. If Vivienne Westwood could cut it, so could Liza. Maybe he'd introduce her to Parkinson. The old rogue had a good eye, and her stuff would be perfect for his Pirelli calendar shoot. Yup, the lovely Liza Grey was one to watch.

As they said their goodbyes, she squeezed his hand and said, 'Why don't you come to Alice's ball? You can be my date.'

'I'd like that very much. When is it?'

'Next Friday — are you free?'

'I'll make sure I am. But what sort of ball — will it be like the club?'

'No, not exactly. The invitation says "dress to excess" so you've got to make an effort. There'll be all kinds of interesting people, you'll see. Alice's parties are always the best. Oh, and you must wear a mask. The more elaborate the better.'

'I'll take that as a challenge.'

'Good, then I'll see you on Friday. Pick me up at eight', she said and kissed him on the cheek.

* * *

Writing is like prospecting: you sometimes sift panfuls of sand before you find a nugget of gold. But sand was threatening to overwhelm him like never before.

He was working on an arts review of the year, charting a course through the cultural highs and lows. The high point? Undoubtedly Howard Hodgkin's galleries at the Biennale — easily the best thing he'd seen for ages. H had painted the walls an elusive shade of green, which somehow managed to draw the fugitive Venetian light deeper into his own colours. It was masterful.

One evening at the Cipriani, H had confided, tongue-in-cheek: 'The only things that ever give me trouble are sex and lighting'. Personally, he'd never had to worry about lighting, but he knew too well what H meant about sex. Trouble was an understatement. Sex filled his horizon; it occluded his vision; it addled his brain. No matter what the topic, his current situation was far more compelling. Socrates himself could not have interrogated the direction of his life more thoroughly than he was at that point.

Damn! The door buzzer sounded, and another nugget eluded him. Damn, damn, damn!

'Hi, it's me, Candy!' She was the last person he expected to hear from, having been so firmly rebuffed before. 'I'm really sorry', she said, 'I was mean to you the other day and I came to apologise.'

She'd had her pink hair styled in a long bob. She looked happy, alert. A bit fuller in the face, possibly, but fabulous, nonetheless. 'I want to tell you why I disappeared', she said, 'but first you must tell *me* something. What made you come looking for me?'

He handed her the video cassette. 'You never came back for Lulu … I knew something must have happened.'

'Oh, I see …' Was that the beginning of a tear? If it was, it must have lost the will and retreated. 'I hope you watched it.'

'I did. More than once, actually.'

'Then I hope you learned something too.'

'That it's a man's world, as you said.'

'Yes, it is … maybe more than even I really understood.' She gave a look that said, 'present company excepted' and dropped the cassette into her bag. 'And now you've got to tell me how you met Jackie. I've been racking my brains, but I can't make the connection.'

'In New York. At the Hellfire.'

'Oh … my … God … Oliver. You are *so* full of surprises.' She sank onto the sofa, as if she'd been dropped from a great height. 'When were you there?'

'A couple of weeks ago. Nola set me up.'

'Well, I never. I had no idea you were so adventurous. You really have been exploring your dark side. I must tell Alice; she'll be so pleased.' He was sure that would not be necessary. 'The Hellfire is the best', Candy continued. 'I still go there if I'm ever in Manhattan, just to keep my hand in.' She closed her fingers into a fist and giggled. 'But you should try Manhole or Mineshaft next time. Boys only though, you might like it.'

He ignored the bait.

'So, what did Jackie say about me?'

'Only that you were old friends.'

'Bless her …'

'Though she did tell me your surname. I could never have found that out by myself.'

'That's also been bugging me. How did you find me? How did you even know where to begin?

He went to the shelf and retrieved the torn envelope. 'You were kind enough to leave me this …'

'Oh, I see … that was silly of me.'

He opened a pack of Gauloises and offered her one. 'Tell me about Jackie', he said. 'She's obviously very fond of you.'

'How much do you know?'

'Only that "she" grew up as a "he" in New Jersey and has an

interesting line in frocks. Oh, and she's got terrific breasts, though I've no idea what they're made of.'

'The tits are probably real … she's had hormone therapy. She's a doll, but her real name is Simon. We met when I was in Manhattan the first time. A group of us used to go to a club in the old Taft Hotel. I found her, I mean him, there one night and we got off. There was a lot of cross-dressing, and he was just amazing, movie-star gorgeous. I had no idea he was a chick with a dick until I got him naked. He was that convincing.'

'Still is … but she's lost the dick.'

'Really? I guess I don't need to ask how you know?'

'I don't suppose it will stay secret for long. We had sex. On top of Jerry's desk, actually.' He heard himself but could barely recognise the voice.

'God, Oliver, I can hardly keep up with you!'

She beamed approval, but he wasn't about to divulge more. 'So, why did it come to an end?' he continued, trying to change the subject.

'It's okay if you don't want to talk about it', she said. 'You can tell me when you're ready.' She paused, drawing on her cigarette, waiting for his next move, but he stayed silent and she relented. 'Simon's a sweet soul. I love him too … I mean her. Sorry, I'm still getting used to the idea. But he was so insecure. All he really wanted was affection. And it's hard to be a dom and make do with vanilla.'

'I've seen your Mapplethorpe portrait', he said. 'Bruce showed me. He says Mapplethorpe found you at the Hellfire, but weren't you too young to be going to a place like that: how did they even let you in?'

'I lifted my skirt if you really want to know. I find it opens most doors. It's kind of win-win.'

Oliver blushed and hoped she hadn't noticed. 'But why didn't you tell me you sat for him? You know it practically confers immortality.'

'I'd sort of forgotten about it. It was a long time ago.'

'Don't you have a print?'

'You *are* joking! Do you have any idea how much they're worth? Thousands, maybe even tens of thousands. I was just a kid, not a celebrity like your friend Bruce. Mapplethorpe didn't have to give me the time of day, never mind anything else. He was cool though. He did let me take one of the Polaroids. But I only had it for about forty-eight hours before my fuck-up of a boyfriend stole it and traded it for H.'

'That's too bad ... do you want to talk about New York?'

'Sure, since we seem to be in the confessional. I suppose it was my initiation. My coming out party. I did things there that I could never have done here. Good and bad.'

'What made you decide to go?'

'I had a huge fight with my mother. I'd been in Paris all summer. When I came back, she went through my things and found my Durex. She went ballistic, threatened to throw me out. So, that night I packed a bag, took fifty quid and her charge card, and caught the bus to Heathrow. The next day I was at JFK.'

'Didn't anyone try to stop you?'

'No, it was easy. No one asked any questions. Even the Amex thing was a piece of cake. My mother and I have the same initials, which helped.'

'What did you do when you got to New York?'

'I didn't know anyone there. I didn't even have a street map. I was clueless, but I got lucky. I met some Punks on the Subway who said I could tag along with them. I don't know why. I must have looked really square. I ended up living in a railroad apartment in Alphabet City.'

'I know the area — it's a slum.'

'It has character. Actually, it has all kinds of things if you look carefully. Some of them quite useful if you're trying to reinvent yourself in a hurry.'

'Such as?'

'Well, I found a shop that sold fetish gear. A real hole-in-the-wall place, run by a creepy old couple — a mom and pop store for weirdos. I bought a leather outfit that I wore to clubs, and a couple of rubber dresses for every day. Within a week I fitted right in. Plus, wearing rubber meant I never had to bother with the laundromat, just rinsed my stuff under the tap. Perfect for a girl on the move.'

'So, how did you discover the Hellfire?'

'That's more complicated. Short version ... I got a tattoo done in an underground place in the East Village. You know it's actually illegal to get a tattoo in New York City. Bizarre. Anyway, the guy who did it was into the scene in a big way. He introduced me. The rest, as they say, is detail.'

'How long did you stay in Manhattan?'

'The first time? About four months. When I broke up with Simon, I was miserable and decided to go home for Christmas. Big mistake. My parents freaked out when they saw me.'

'Why, what happened?'

'Well, first of all, they were pissed off with me for disappearing like that and not getting in touch. The only way they kept track of me was through the Amex bills. Luckily, my dad kept on paying them. Then, on Christmas Eve, my mother walked in while I was showing my sister my piercings.'

'I can imagine that being awkward. Is your sister much younger than you?'

'No, we're twins. I was the second one out, the nasty surprise. We're identical, but you'd never know, we're such different personalities. My mother calls me a degenerate, says I'm a bad influence. I like to think so too, but my sister's practically a saint. She's married now ... banker husband, horses, dogs, Essex farmhouse, the whole deal. Boring beyond belief.'

'Do you see much of your family?'

'My sister, yes. My mother, no. I haven't seen or spoken to her since she threw me out. But I get on pretty well with my dad. We meet for lunch now and then, though I've no idea whether he tells my mother or not.'

'What does your father do?'

'He's a Lloyd's broker. He should've chucked it in yonks ago. But he comes up every morning on the train. I think he must hate it at home almost as much as I did.'

'And your grandparents?'

'All gone, sadly. My grandpa left me the mews house. He was a real sweetie.'

'Was he a broker too?'

'No, he was a bit of a buccaneer. He had one of the first Mercedes dealerships over here. He said German cars and German women were the best in the world. Neither one would ever let you down.'

'Was your grandmother German?'

'Yeah, Poppy met her in Stuttgart at the end of the war. He was stationed over there, helping them rebuild. Apparently, she refused to sleep with him because they weren't married, so he asked her there and then. They got hitched a few days later.'

'He sounds like quite a character.'

'He was. He adored women and they loved him. That's why he had the mews — to get away from the wagging tongues in Essex.'

'Is that where you grew up?'

'Yeah, in the middle of nowhere. But it was different then. I don't belong there now.'

Candy made a silent play of drawing on her cigarette, but he didn't feel like giving up. He'd tapped into too rich a seam. 'Strange that you never bumped into Alice in New York', he said.

'Why do you say that?' she asked, a little too defensively. He could be on dangerous ground.

'Oh, I think somebody said you met in London.'

'Did Alice tell you that?'

'She might have.'

'She was probably trying to throw you off the scent. New York is where we first met. We used to hang out in the same clubs, but she ran with a different crowd. She had a photographer boyfriend who didn't like me very much. I think he suspected her of trying to get into my pants.'

'And was she?'

'I don't know, I never found out.' Hmm, not the whole story. 'Alice is a very difficult person to get close to', she said after another pause.

'In what way?'

'Well, for one thing you can easily get burned. I think most people disappoint her in the end. And she can be quite cruel if you don't measure up. Very cruel.' Her cigarette extinguished, she lapsed into silence.

'You mentioned Paris. Were you there on holiday?'

'God no, I was staying with friends of my parents in the 6th.

It was all very smart. I was supposed to be polishing my French, but I spent most of the time mooching about with their son, Clément, smoking dope and having sex. It was his first time too, so we made it up as we went along. We'd sneak out and go to all-night cinemas and watch porn movies. Stuff like that.'

'What did you see?'

'Anything we could find. We saw *Emmanuelle* a million times. I had the hots for Daniel Sarky, and Clément fancied Sylvia Kristel, so we kept going back. We saw *Maîtresse* a few times too. It gave us all kinds of ideas, not that we got the chance to explore many of them.'

'I went to see *Maîtresse* a couple of years ago at the Scala,' he said. 'I read it had been censored, but even so it got pretty close to the bone.'

Candy smiled at the unintended pun. 'You're right, it's a bit raw in places, but the French never seem to mind.'

'Were you in love with the French boy?'

'God no! It was just physical.'

'Have you ever been in love?'

'Have you?' she countered.

'No, I don't think so.' Now who was lying?

'You'll know when it happens. It impacts on all the senses, physically and mentally. You can't sleep; you can't eat; you can't focus on anything else. It's the most unsettling and thrilling thing you'll ever experience.' He recognised the symptoms immediately. 'How many times has it happened?'

'Just once …'

'Would you like to tell me about it?'

'Not now, I'm not ready.' Her turn to blush. 'I came here to tell you another story.'

She explained her relationship with Margrét and how she had set up the appointment with Diessel: 'She hates me. It's obvious now, but I never noticed. I assumed she was just moping, but it turned out she was plotting.'

She recounted the experience in the hotel and how mortified she'd felt on being confronted by the manager. She explained the effect the attack had had on her; the sense of failure it had induced and how she'd hidden herself away. Finally, she rolled down her tights and made him touch the scars on her legs: like Christ showing Thomas his wounds. Then, apparently mid-flow, she stopped talking and got up. 'I didn't mean to stay so long. I must go … I've things to do.'

She hugged him tight. 'You're a sweet boy, Oliver. You know that don't you? But there's really no need to worry about me. I'll be fine. Okay?'

He realised that she'd rekindled their friendship and that she would probably visit again. She had her mojo back and he was happy for her.

33

'No Oliver, it sounds like a Fellini', said Jan dismissively, when he told him about Nola and Irina. He could tell Jan was enjoying the story, but however much detail he filled in, and more significantly, how much he omitted, Jan would not concede that Nola existed beyond the realms of his fevered imagination. 'I don't believe it', he said, suspicious as ever. 'She is *too* good to be true. You have been watching *La Dolce Vita*.'

'I'll introduce you, then you'll see.' And so it went on. But Jan had a point. Oliver did sometimes feel as if he'd been cast alongside Anita Ekberg. As if he should be so lucky. The only problem was that the screenplay hadn't been finished, so he had no idea how his role was meant to develop. Or whether the movie would turn out to be a romance or a farce. He was just playing it scene-by-scene as fate directed, half expecting the credits to roll at any minute. He wanted to believe that Nola was serious, but all the evidence pointed in the opposite direction. He hadn't seen her since their parting kiss in the Savoy. Most likely he'd failed the screen test and been written out of the script.

Everybody talks about closure, though he knew no such thing was possible. Life is simply one long-drawn-out ambiguity, an evolving tableau. His only certainty was exhaustion — physical, emotional, financial. He was running on empty. He had to decide, even if it meant forcing her hand.

He shouldn't have come. He felt like a stalker, or a crummy private dick, creeping about, spying on her, invading her territory. But here he was, full circle, back at Bon-Bon. He opened the doors on a party in full swing. The tables were full, and the big room was buzzing. Even the skinny kid at the keyboard was doing his best to channel Fats Waller.

He took a seat at the bar and ordered a scotch. It took a minute or two to locate Nola. She was at a corner table, almost hidden behind the piano. With her on the banquette was a fifty-something John; pudgy, vaguely Far Eastern. The guy spoke, and she reacted a little too enthusiastically; he touched her arm, and she allowed his hand to rest there a little too long. It was obvious where they were heading, assuming they hadn't been there already.

The cigarette girl stopped at the bar for a refill. He'd been observing her too. Her hair was set in a tight perm and her tutu flattered legs that were otherwise too short for her body. She was enchanting. Or perhaps he just needed enchantment.

'Busy tonight', he said.

'It always is at Christmas. That's how Santa stays so jolly. He knows where all the bad girls live.'

'I'm Oliver … what's your name?'

'Cigarette Girl', she replied and curtseyed, dipping her tray in salute.

'Really? Your parents must have been incredibly farsighted.'

'Uncannily so …'

Replenished, she set off on another circuit. He watched her push her way back into the throng, then he finished his scotch and ordered another. She was back in twenty minutes, fresh out of cigars. 'So, what are you called when you're not selling cigarettes?'

'Expensive …'

He chuckled and saw the beginnings of a smile. 'What if I said my name was Millionaire?'

'Then you can call me Petra.'

'And Multi-millionaire?'

'Petra honey …'

'You know you're much too smart to be selling cigarettes.'

'And you don't look dumb enough to be sitting here alone, getting drunk.'

'Touché!'

By her third stop, he was prepared. 'Petra, would you mind doing me a little favour?' She looked at him quizzically: 'Clothes on or clothes off?'

'Would you give this to the girl sitting by the piano?'

'Oh, you mean Nola. How disappointing. I hoped it would be clothes off.' He folded the note in half and gave it to her. Then he slid a fiver into the corner of her tray. 'Am I supposed to wait for a reply?'

'No, that's not necessary, thanks.'

Petra handed over the paper and pointed towards the bar. Nola read the message but didn't look up.

Thirty minutes later she left with Mister Asia-Pacific. He was a full head shorter than her, dumpy, with a complexion like a pineapple, but he had a swagger that told you he was loaded or hung like a horse. Most likely both. Quite a coup for the little fella, no doubt, but just another trick for hostess Nola.

Mille e tre! If she'd been with three men a week for seven years, which was quite possible, given what he'd just seen, she'd be well past 1,003 by now. So, what did that make her? No, he might hate her for it, but he had no right to judge. She owed him nothing, not even his dignity. That was his alone to squander.

'Back again …' Petra was his new best friend. 'What was all that about; how do you know Nola?'

'Well, it's a long story, with a rotten ending. Kind of a cat and mouse caper, without the laughs.'

'And I'm guessing you're the mouse, right?'

'I'm afraid so …'

He drained his glass and set it on the counter. 'Now tell me, I've been trying to imagine the worst pick-up line you've ever heard.'

'You've struck lucky, or it's my lucky strike. I must have heard it a thousand times and every one of them thinks he's a real wit.'

'Good, now I know what to avoid … and the best?'

'What time do you finish? That usually works.'

She was delightful, exactly what he needed. 'So, what time *do* you finish?'

'About one usually. Depends how soon everyone else goes home.'

He looked at his watch — eleven fifty-five. 'Come and find me when you're ready. I'll be here.'

'You do know this is strictly professional, right?'

'I'm sorry. I hadn't realised. How stupid of me.'

'Everything in this place has a ticket, sweetheart', she said. 'Even the piano player if that's what turns you on. Probably have the piano tuner too if you can find him.'

'How much?'

'Thirty for the first hour, a hundred for the night.'

'Okay, but I'll have to stop and get some cash. I think there's a machine on the way to the car.'

'Where's your hotel?'

'Oh, I don't have one … we can go back to my place.'

'Sorry handsome, I don't do that. Ask me again when you've got a room.' She gestured to the barman: 'Antonio here can help you. His brother's the concierge at the Park Tower.' Antonio had been listening. What else would you expect from a barman? 'If you like, I call Franco', he said, filling Oliver's glass.

'No, I have another idea. Where can I make a call?'

'Hello?' He let the coins drop in the box. 'Liza, it's me, Oliver. Look, I know it's late, but I'd really like to see you. I need to talk. Can I come over?'

'I'd love to see you too, but it's not that convenient right now.' She sounded preoccupied.

'*Who is it?*' He recognised Alice's voice in the background.

'*Oliver*', she said, her hand muffling the receiver, '*He sounds drunk.*'

'Look, don't worry. I understand … I'll see you on Friday', he said, and hung up. He turned to get his coat, but the opening bars of Thelonius Monk's *'Round Midnight* and a craving for female company drew him back downstairs.

187

* * *

Arriving home in the morning he found the light on his answering machine glowing red. Knowing what it meant, he didn't react immediately. First, he made a pot of coffee — stronger than usual — then lit a cigarette. Eventually he pressed 'play'.

'Ollie, it's Nola. I don't think I can see you again. It's been lovely. I'm really sorry ...'

He ran the message again, just to be sure. Then twice more. Then he dialled her number, but her machine clicked in straight away. 'So, this is how it ends', he said, addressing the room. In a way he was surprised it hadn't happened sooner. Their affair had lasted barely six weeks, and they'd spent as many nights together. It had been just another diversion for her; a charade. But it could have been worse. She might have dumped him by fax. Or post. Or carrier pigeon. Or, like Candy, simply vanished and said nothing at all.

34

Oliver pulled up outside Liza's studio promptly at eight and sounded the horn. She climbed into the Porsche and was consumed almost immediately by the folds of her greatcoat. 'I thought you'd be late', she said, 'but I was ready just in case.'

'Punctuality is one of my vices', he replied.

'We've got loads of time. Let's go somewhere first so I can take a proper look at you. How about the Colony? I haven't been there for weeks.'

'I don't think I can risk the Colony dressed like this, do you?' he said. 'I have a better idea. There's a party at the AA tonight. We could drop in there.'

'Alcoholics Anonymous?'

'Ha ha ... no, its ugly stepsister, the Architectural Association. It's only five minutes away and we don't have to stop long. I think you'll like it ... there'll be plenty of champagne.'

'You forget, I don't drink.'

'Oh, I'm sorry. How stupid of me.'

'Stop apologising and let's go. I'd like to meet your friends.'

He parked in Bedford Square and got out to open the door for her.

'Good manners — is that another of your failings?' she asked.

'I know, I'm a lost cause. You should probably leave your coat in the car. It's bound to be hot in there.'

She slipped it off and flung it onto the seat.

'Wow, you look amazing', he said, when he'd taken in the full effect. Her dress was a sculptural masterpiece, with a laced back and a peplum waist whose folds bobbed almost weightlessly above a tapered skirt.

'Do you like it? It took ages to figure out the pattern. It's difficult to walk in though. If we're going far, you'll have to undo me a bit.' He obliged, and pulled up the zipper, somehow managing to resist her shiny black legs.

The front door of the AA was flung wide open, and the sounds of the Stones' *Satisfaction* cannoned down the stairs. He guided Liza up to the first floor, hanging back just enough to observe her progress. 'This way', he said, when they reached the bar. You could see why so many architects ended up living in period houses when they insisted on schooling themselves in fine Georgian rooms such as this. 'Now let's see if we can find you something non-alcoholic. I won't be a minute.'

'I can feel a dozen pairs of eyes undressing me', she said, when he returned.

'That's probably a conservative estimate', he replied, handing her a glass. 'Soda water with a dash of lime ... I'm afraid it's the best I could do.'

'It's as if they've never seen a woman before.'

'Well, they probably haven't seen one quite as exotic as you.'

'Who's that man, grinning at you like an idiot?' asked Liza. Jan was making his way towards them, clearly unable to contain his amusement, a bouncing Czech. He looked Oliver up and down.

'I didn't know it was fancy dress', he said. If he'd smirked much more, his face would have split in half.

189

'Very funny. We're going on to a ball, so I've brought my tails out of retirement.'

'It must be a rubber ball', said Jan, stroking Liza's sleeve. And then in a stage whisper, 'Is this one of your wicked women?'

'Liza, this is Jan, who used to be one of my most distinguished friends.'

'Are you one of the mysterious girls Oliver's told me so much about? He doesn't normally let us meet his girlfriends, although I'm sure he has hundreds. He's so secretive ...'

'I'm sorry about that, he's incorrigible', Oliver said, when Jan had finally taken the hint and moved on. 'I'm rather fond of him, but he doesn't know when to shut up.'

Liza shrugged: 'I liked him. He's quite charming.'

'Oh, hello Cedric ... good party!' said Oliver, cheerfully.

'Well, I've never been to a *bad* party, dear boy. Have you?' said Cedric, brandy glass in hand, hovering longer than necessary. 'I think you should introduce me to your delightful friend. I hear you've been having quite an adventure recently. How was New York?'

Okay, so everyone knew. Jan was such a garrulous bastard. Liza gripped his arm, a look of horror on her face.

'Oliver, there's a hand on my bottom, and I can see it's not yours.'

'Oh Christ, not another one. All the architects I've ever met have been oversexed. Oversexed and under-resourced. Shall we go?'

They drove eastwards along the Embankment, the traffic crawling forward slowly, and the streetlights playing warily in the puddles in the road.

'You made quite an impression just now', he said. 'But you need to fill me in a bit more, so I can introduce you properly next time.'

'How much more?' she asked, obviously not keen.

'Let's start with where you grew up.'

'In Oldham, in a great big Catholic family. I went to church and said my prayers on Sunday. I was very happy, and not much happened until I started art school.'

'Where was that?'

'St Martin's. I did foundation then fashion.'

'I guessed as much … and then?'

'Then I went to Paris and learned how to cut patterns and sew stitches as fine as the hairs on butterfly wings. But that's chapter two …' She gazed out of the window, as reticent as Nola was voluble.

'So where did you work in Paris?'

'Pierre Cardin's studio.'

'Oh really! How interesting. Now you mention it, I can see the connection. His work is all about structure, just like yours. He could have been an architect … except he's much more interesting than most architects.'

'Cardin's a genius. I learned a huge amount. The big thing he taught me is not to overload a piece with too many ideas. You need to edit.'

'I think a lot of designers would benefit from that advice.'

She fell quiet and he tried again: 'So how long did you work for Cardin?'

'Just over a year.'

'And how did you get the job? It can't have been easy.'

'Actually, it was simple. I just turned up one day with my portfolio and rang the bell. There's a lovely woman, Francine, who runs the workroom. She took me in and looked after me. I think I was sort of her mascot.'

'And what's he like, Cardin?'

'I don't really know. Everyone in the studio is in awe of him. But I don't think he even noticed I was there. It's like any fashion house. He only talks to André and a few other people, and they only talk to certain other people, and so on.'

'Sounds like the *Telegraph* … who's André?'

'André Oliver, Cardin's artistic director. You never hear about him, but he's an incredible designer in his own right.'

'And the workroom … how was that?'

'Long hours, manic deadlines, terrible pay.'

'Still sounds like the *Telegraph*.'

'I don't believe that. I'm sure you're doing very nicely. Alice has told me all about you.'

'Now you're making me nervous. What did she say?'

'She seems to think you're some sort of dilettante ... that writing is just an extension of your social life.'

'Did she really say that?'

'Not in those exact words. But she said all the genuine writers she's known have been manic depressives ...'

'Well, that's probably true, but then she hasn't met Bruce.'

'... and that you're obviously having too much fun.'

He took that as a rebuke for having interrupted her in the studio. She must think he had nothing better to do than swan around all day, making social calls, when other people had to earn a living. True, he'd only ever had a casual acquaintance with the Protestant work ethic, but writing had always been a source of pleasure, so he'd never thought of it in other terms.

They followed the river until the road turned inland, then headed towards Wapping and the lifeless old docks.

'So, what brought you back to London?'

'Well, I was homesick, I suppose; and I have a sort of love-hate relationship with the city. I love Paris but can't stand the Parisians. They're so flippin' lah-di-dah.'

'I can't tell you how many times I've heard that. You know the Roman name for Paris was *Lutetia* — it translates roughly as *swamp*.'

'That's funny! I didn't know the Romans had a sense of humour.'

'I'm sorry, I interrupted you: so, what did you do when you came back?'

'Well, I have a friend, John Sutcliffe, who runs AtomAge — he makes rubber clothing, but not the sort of thing you can wear every day — and he promised to help me if I ever took the plunge. So, I worked there for six months. That's how I got started. I would never have managed it by myself.'

'That was generous of him.'

'John's amazing. He showed me how to seal seams, gave me pieces to make, introduced me to clients ... you'd be surprised how many famous people have a naughty little secret. He'll probably be there tonight. You can meet him.'

192

'So where does that take us up to?'

'To the end of chapter two.'

'And chapter three?'

'Chapter three doesn't have a conclusion yet ...'

The narrow street was lined on both sides with cars. As he got out of the Porsche a taxi pulled up, then another, and another.

'Did you bring your mask?' Liza asked.

'Yes, it's Venetian. Quite old I think, maybe even antique. But it's spent most of its life in an attic.' He reached into the car and retrieved it from behind the seat — a Janus mask of traditional pattern, reflecting good and evil, comedy and tragedy. He held it to his face.

'Perfect! It suits you.'

'Now let's see yours.'

Liza opened her bag and took out what looked like a delicate bird with outspread wings, fashioned from glossy black feathers. 'Here ... be careful or it will take your eye out.'

Alice was waiting to greet them, dressed in the slippery white gown that he'd last seen in pieces on Liza's table. She wore a double string of pearls and held up a delicate porcelain mask that made her look like a china doll.

'Welcome', she said and blew them both kisses. 'I hope you'll find plenty to amuse you. We've tried to think of everything ...' The consummate hostess, mistress of ceremonies, Queen of the Night.

The Velvet Underground cut seamlessly to *Die Walküre* and Brünnhilde's desperate plea to Wotan. Not music to dance to exactly, but scene setting. Before them was the vast expanse of an abandoned warehouse. A skin floor, appropriately, one of those secret places that the city only reveals long after they have died. Searchlights ringed one long aisle, sending narrow beams up through the smoky air, like Wotan's magic fire. Braziers glowed and chestnuts roasted; suspended figures moved lazily in the updraught; and everywhere, a sea of shiny figures ebbed and flowed: the kinky cognoscenti, the fetish aristocracy.

'Who are all these people?' he asked.

'A mix … all of Alice's friends will be here. And friends of friends. And people from Submission and Maitresse and the other clubs. Everyone we know, really.'

A waiter offered champagne or orange juice. Plump little twists of rice paper were arranged around the edge of the tray, like sweets. 'What are these?' he asked, picking one up.

'Christmas snow bombs', said Liza. 'I'm surprised you need to ask.'

'Oh, I see. No thanks.

'I can't do it either if that makes you feel any better.'

'Who paid for all this — not Alice surely?'

'No, are you kidding? Alice hasn't got a cent. But there are plenty of people on the scene who'll reach into their pockets if they think they can have some fun.'

A girl in a transparent catsuit brushed against him and he touched her arm. The rubber concealed nothing, but made her skin feel smooth and flawless, as if it had been dipped in oil. He watched her fluid progress across the room.

'It's a bacchanal', he said. 'Crossed with the seven circles of Hell.'

'I'm glad you approve … let's explore.'

Alice had invited a rope master from Osaka and a rope mistress from Manhattan, who commanded opposite ends of the long space. Assistants were on hand to help with undressing, and clothes were arranged on rails. He watched as the master hoisted a girl slowly into the air. Her breasts hung free between the ropes and little bells on her piercings tinkled as she moved.

'And she shall have music wherever she goes.'

Liza appeared not to hear. 'He's an artist', she said. 'Look how beautifully he works the rope.' The master made a slight adjustment, lifting the girl's legs higher. When he'd finished, Liza approached him and asked, 'Master, will you please bind me?'

'*Korewa koei ni omoimasu*', said the old man, bowing deeply: 'It will be an honour.' Liza unlaced the back of her dress and Oliver leaned forward to help with the zip. She did a little dance and wiggled her hips and the dress slithered to the floor, leaving her in rubber stockings and the tiniest of thongs. He shivered on her behalf.

194

Standing too close to the wall of speakers, he nearly jumped out of his skin as Violetta's spirited aria from *La Traviata* met the explosive force of the New York Dolls' *Rainbow Store*. It was an inspired, if unpredictable segue.

'Sounds like they're playing your song ...'

He turned around to find a slim figure clad head-to-toe in red rubber, the polished surface shimmering like a rich copper glaze. A hood squeezed her mouth into a lipsticky pout. 'It's me, Candy!' she said, shouting to be heard. 'Love the handbag darlin'. You accessorise well.'

He looked at the studded leather clutch bag and held it up for inspection. 'It's not mine, it's Liza's. I'm supposed to be looking after it for her.'

'A pity. I'm not sure I want to believe you. It makes you look so much more interesting. And what have you done with Liza?'

'She's over there, otherwise engaged', he said, pointing. Liza was suspended on her side, caught in what looked like a fragment of a spider's web, one leg hooked above the other, swinging slowly. She looked serenely happy.

'Alice told me that she wanted to tie *you* up at Maitresse, but you wouldn't let her. Says you ran off like a frightened rabbit. Is that right?'

'It's partly true ... I wasn't quite ready.'

'You know you should let yourself go a bit more. There's a whole world of experiences to enjoy.'

'I *am* trying', he said, wishing Liza were there to defend him.

'I saw the two of you arrive', Candy continued. 'You make a fine couple. She's far more suitable than your previous girlfriend.'

'Is Nola here?'

'I haven't seen her, but that's the beauty of a masked ball. You can be invisible if you like.'

'You look fabulous, by the way', he said.

'Oh, thank you. These are just some of my old work clothes. I didn't feel like dressing up.'

He chuckled and she whipped him hard on the thigh. 'Ouch! What was that for?'

'Lesson one: never laugh at the Mistress!'

'I'm sorry ...' Swoosh. Her crop landed a second time. 'You can do better than that ... mind your manners!'

'I'm sorry, *Mistress*!'

'That's *much* better. Now kiss the whip!' He did as he was told. 'Now say *thank you*.'

'Thank you, Mistress.'

'Good, you're learning. Now come with me. I want to introduce you to a friend of mine. She's an extremely strict disciplinarian. I have a hunch you're going to like her.'

Candy guided him to a remote corner, where a selection of medieval-looking equipment lay waiting, like a scene from the *Hammer House of Horror*. In the middle of it all, standing guard, was an Emma Peel lookalike in a leather jumpsuit.

'This is Mistress Phoebe', Candy said; 'Mistress, this is Oliver. He requires the most severe form of correction.'

'I can see that', said the Mistress, prodding his balls with her cane.

'But before you begin, you must have a safeword', Candy explained. 'Sometimes people say "stop" during a session and don't really mean it. They can get quite difficult about it afterwards. But if you use the safeword, the Mistress will know what to do.'

'What sort of word?'

'Short is best. Mistress Phoebe can select one for you, but it's better if you choose your own. Then you won't forget it.'

'Rimbaud', he said. *Ram-bo*. He wasn't sure whether the pun had registered, but it made him smile anyway.

35

Alice's plan was working to perfection. She'd put the word out through her various networks that the party had 'potential'. To the Berliners who ran Gore, the club patronised by Pedersen, she presented it as an opportunity to harvest new blood, and maybe enjoy a little recreational bondage into the bargain. What's not to like? Their circle had kept to the secluded parts of the warehouse, where they remained undisturbed.

The only real unknown had been whether Pedersen would be drawn into the trap. Alice had stationed herself at the entrance so that she could monitor who came in. At 10.25 he arrived alone, dressed for battle in khaki latex combat gear. He wore a patch over one eye, like a rubberised Moshe Dayan. A nod from Alice, and from thereon he'd been tailed wherever he went.

So far so good. But Candy hadn't been at all convinced that he would play ball. He was a slippery fucker. Then shortly after one o'clock she saw him approach Mistress Nemesis — a nice detail on Alice's part — and watched as he was hogtied. He couldn't have done it better if they'd shown him the script. She drew particular pleasure from the nature of his punishment.

The mistress was fulfilling her role elegantly. Having trussed him securely and fitted him with a padded leather hood, which made all aural and visual contact quite impossible, she was slowly hoisting him far into the upper reaches of the roof. And doubtless to his great consternation, that was where he was destined to remain.

The human body can run quite efficiently for weeks without food, but after three days without water, dehydration becomes critical. First the skin starts to itch, the lips crack and weep, and the tongue begins to swell. Then the eyes gradually slow in their sockets, the blood grows thicker, the heart protests and muscles scream. Cognitive function falters, then fails, the onset of delirium marking the final slide into unconsciousness.

In the cold winter air, his body would slowly dehydrate with every breath. And as he struggled, the ropes would chafe his flesh until it was raw. Sleep or death: eventually he wouldn't care which came first. And nor did Candy. One phone call to Paddington Green on Monday morning and he'd be in custody. The coppers could stop off at Alice's and prise Margrét out of her hidey-hole too. It was beautiful, and no more than they deserved.

Candy rewarded herself with a cigarette. A lungful of toxins seemed appropriate at this point.

36

'Okay, pretty boy, I'm ready to go', said Liza, draping her arms around Oliver's neck. 'It's way past my bedtime!'

'Shall I take you home?'

'I thought you'd never ask. I've been waiting for you to make a move.'

'I'm sorry, I'm a bit slow. I wish you'd given me more of a signal.'

'I did try, that first night in the club.'

'I was a little nervous that evening', he said, battling with the strings on his mask. 'I must have missed it.' He drew her closer and kissed her on the mouth. She responded, and he slid his hand over a breast, locating a firm nipple beneath the warm rubber. He pinched it, gently at first, then harder.

'Yow!' she cried: 'Let's go.'

He drove rapidly through the deserted byways of the city, the rasp of the Porsche's air-cooled engine and the rhythmic slap of the windscreen wipers providing the dominant soundtrack. Liza was fast asleep, snoring softly. It was an unexpectedly sweet scene.

'Nola's a heartbreaker, a serial offender', Alice had said earlier. And when he'd protested, she'd forced home the point: 'Look, I love her dearly, but she's a sex junkie. And she's a romance junkie too, which makes life far more complicated for everyone. Often, I don't think she even knows she's doing it. You're just her latest victim, that's all. You must try not to take it personally.'

He was amazed at how people invariably morphed into their parents. Not so long ago he would have run a mile from the prospect of a serious relationship. Now he had begun to crave one.

Liza lived above her workroom, up another creaking flight of stairs. The flat was cold and spartan: bare floorboards and no blinds, no art, no inessentials. The bed was a futon mattress unfurled on a pallet on the floor, Japanese style, with a duvet covered in black cotton.

He peered into the narrow courtyard, but all the other windows were dark, their curtains drawn. He couldn't stop shivering.

If anything, it was colder in her room than it had been outside. It was the home of a woman who positively embraced discomfort. But he shouldn't complain. At least he wouldn't have to foot another hotel bill.

'Hey, you ... hurry up and unzip me!'

'Sorry, I was dreaming.'

He pulled the zipper up as far as it would go and ran his fingers beneath the material, which was moist to the touch. She shook off the dress and he bent down and kissed her back, drawing his lips slowly down her spine.

'Wait ...' She pulled away, tugging at her thong. It dropped into a heap with her dress, and she darted beneath the duvet. 'Quick! Get into bed before my butt freezes.' He looked in vain for somewhere to hang his tailcoat and she pelted him with her rolled-up stockings: 'Come *on* ...'

He was woken by the sound of an ancient boiler coming reluctantly to life; water gurgled noisily in the radiator beside the bed. Liza was fast asleep, lying on her back with one arm raised on the pillow. He nuzzled her ear, enjoying her warmth against his cheek. Her hair smelt faintly of chestnuts and Eau de Cologne.

Sex with Nola had been poised, balletic. It had an aesthetic dimension. With her, he was the focus of a command performance. Liza, in contrast, made love as if she had an insatiable hunger for pleasure; she devoured him, and he was surprised how much he enjoyed it. He was strangely protective of her, his beautiful cheap date.

Liza's rubber dress had formed itself into a pool on the floor. He picked it up and was amazed how heavy it was, and how cold it felt without her inside it. He gathered up his things, and taking care not to disturb her, tiptoed downstairs. It had been nagging since he first met her, but now he'd placed the name:

Oh, fare you well, Miss Liza Gray, I'm afraid your heart will break,
When you hears tell that I am lost in the Lady of the Lake

It was a piece of doggerel retained from schooldays. Strange how the mind works. He dressed silently, folded his tie, and put it in his pocket. He didn't want to go without saying goodbye, nor did he want to wait until she woke up, but he had no way of leaving a note. And the flat wasn't much help either. Then he had an idea. On his way out he stopped in the workroom; the transaction took less than a minute. How long would it take her to notice that her mannequin had acquired a white tie?

37

Monday's post brought a seasonal mix of cards and final demands, plus the letter from the bank that he'd been dreading. Playing relationship roulette with Nola had emptied his account and exhausted his overdraft. Now, full of Christmas cheer, they wanted their money back.

He fanned out the remaining envelopes: clearly a rotten hand. Only one looked inviting — crisp, blue, and perfumed. He sliced it open with a kitchen knife. Inside was one of the shortest letters he'd ever seen:

What did my fingers do before they held you?
What did my heart do, with its love?

But then again, he'd never received a love letter, so he was hardly an expert. He knew enough, though, to identify the source: *Three Women*, a poem by Sylvia Plath. At least Nola hadn't lost her sense of humour. He checked the postmark. It had been franked on the same day he'd barged into Bon Bon. She must have posted it that afternoon on her way to work. Ugh, another novice move on his part. His stupidity knew no bounds. No wonder she was angry.

He replayed Nola's phone message over again in his head. She'd said, 'I don't *think* I can see you again.' Not 'I don't *want* to see you again.' Perhaps she hadn't given up entirely. He held the envelope to his nose, anticipating her familiar scent, but all he got was Smythson.

Curiously, Nola's bullet had also killed his writing demons and allowed him to resume work on his novel. He assumed his familiar position at the typewriter and fed a fresh sheet of paper into the machine.

When the house he lived in was built, his living room would have been the master bedroom. The bed would have stood where he had his dining table, opposite the hearth. He pictured a fire, banked up for the night, and a couple making love as he sat invisibly in the room, his distance as voyeur enforced not by space but by the passage of time. He imagined whispered conversation, and the hushed acoustics of the room. Everyone was familiar with the idea of ghosts from the past, but what about ghosts from the future?

That was the essence of the story. Trouble was, he was haunted by the spirits of countless other writers. All the memorable first lines of all the novels he'd ever read jostled together on the page, and the longer he waited for them to disperse, the harder it was to start.

There is nothing to writing, said Hemingway. All you do is sit at a typewriter and bleed. Perhaps if he just kept hitting the keys, something meaningful would emerge. He tried not to focus too much, to allow the words to flow freely and find their own order. The constant memory of Nola's silky legs provided the perfect diversion.

Hello, he spied Candy in the street below and signalled to come up. 'Promise me you're not armed', he said, when he opened the door.

Candy looked mischievous. 'I hope you enjoyed yourself on Friday', she said. 'Mistress Phoebe certainly did.'

'I rather got that impression.'

'She asked me to give you this, so you'll know how to find her when you're ready for more.' It was Phoebe's card, the usual pattern.

'Hmm … I'll think about that.' He picked up Nola's letter and toyed with it absentmindedly, turning it over and over. 'Have you ever met someone you'd like to spend the rest of your life with?'

'Isn't this a conversation we've had before?'

'No, I'm not talking about love. I'm not sure I know what that is. I mean a soulmate. Someone on your own wavelength; when you feel you're more complete in someone's company than you are without them. That they challenge you in ways that are good for you.'

'I'm guessing we're talking in the past tense here?'

'The recent past.'

'I thought so. You should try to get over her.'

'That's what Alice said.'

'Well Alice knows her better than most. But somehow, I can't see you two growing old together. You're far too gentle and she's permanently on heat. She'd give you the runaround. You'd end up being miserable.'

'But apart from that Mrs Lincoln, how did you enjoy the play?'

'Sorry, I didn't mean to be so blunt. But you know it's true.'

'Except that deep down I think that she feels the same way I do.'

'You know I may just get Phoebe to give you another going over for being so dumb. What about Liza? You two are perfect together.'

'You think so?'

'Yes!'

'Well, I'm completely confused. Read this …'

Candy unfolded the letter. 'Oh, I see. You'd better pour me a drink. Make that non-alcoholic.'

'It's a quote from Sylvia Plath', he said. 'But it's not as straightforward as it seems. Plath was referring to a baby.'

'Do you think she knows that?'

'I'm sure she does. Everything Nola does is nuanced in some way.'

'Hmm, somehow I can't see her suckling a brat.'

'She told me she'd had an abortion. The child would be nine in January. She told me that too. She even has a name for him: Tom, after Tom Thumb, because that's how big he was at eleven weeks.'

'That's really creepy. Anyway, how does she know it wasn't a girl?' Candy placed a hand on her stomach and let it rest there.

'She doesn't. I think she just pictures herself with a boy. She tries to pretend she doesn't care. She calls him her dirty little bastard, but I can tell she's still grieving.'

'You think she wants to have a kid with you?'

'Well, it's not so unusual. I've seen it happen to women her age.' Candy didn't respond, but he could tell that she was holding something back. 'You think she's messing with me, don't you?'

'I wouldn't rule it out. Your sweet Nola has form.'

38

Oliver loathed Christmas and had done so from his teens. It was the absolute zero of the bachelor's calendar, the bleakest of social landscapes. His choices so far were limited. Either the wasteland that was lunch with his parents, or an overnight with cousins in the frozen tundra of Norfolk.

The second option didn't sound so bad until one factored in the stress of dealing with their friends and their friends' kids. There is no civilised way of dining with small children. They kill conversation and all the other pleasures of the table. Plus, he'd be the only adult sleeping alone. The one viable course would be to hit the bottle on Christmas morning and keep going. He imagined his hosts' whispered conversation:

'Have you noticed, Oliver's drinking *very* heavily?'

'I wonder if he's ever going to settle down.'

'You know, I've never seen him with a woman.' Etcetera, etcetera.

Even his father suspected he was 'queer', although, typically, he used a quaint formulation: 'highly unlikely to have children'.

Maybe he should invite Liza. That would certainly stir things up. But it might be more fun to take her home to his parents, just to torment his mother. She'd be mortified. He could hear her, complaining to his father: 'Why has Oliver brought that dreadful girl? And what on earth is she wearing?'

No, Liza would hate it. Far better to take her away somewhere; preferably somewhere warm. Or stay in town and book into a hotel, have Christmas on room service. A pity he'd broken the bank. Perhaps Christmas in the flat wouldn't be so bad. They could buy a tree and decorate it together. Roast a goose. It would be cosy, *gemütlich*. Assuming that he was feeling better.

He had practically been born a hypochondriac and so didn't underestimate the power of autosuggestion, but the fact was that at some point since his evening with Bruce he'd begun to feel out of sorts. It began with a sore throat, then his bones began to ache; he had night sweats and felt lethargic.

'You may get dressed now Mr Woolf', said the doctor. 'I detect a slight fever and your lymph nodes are raised, but nothing more serious. It's possible that it is mononucleosis, although unlikely if you contracted it as a child.'

'I'm sorry, should I know what that is?'

'Mononucleosis … glandular fever. It's highly infectious, but infection can only be passed through direct physical contact … kissing usually.'

'Oh, I see. No, I haven't had it before.'

'I'm going to send a blood sample for testing. The lab generally takes a week or thereabouts, so we should have a clearer picture after the Christmas break. In the meantime, I recommend complete bed rest. Do you have someone who can look after you?'

'I'm afraid not.'

'No relatives you can stay with?'

'None at all', he said, certain that he'd rather die than rely on his mother's tender mercy.

Walking back to the flat, he paused at the window of the little café where he sometimes stopped for an espresso. No, it couldn't be? 'Nola!' He rapped on the glass, and she spun around, startled. He smiled and mouthed 'sorry', and she waved back. The girl seemed nice, whoever she was. Only then did he realise the strength of his connection with Nola and how much he missed her.

There is a moment in the *Phaedo* where Socrates observes, *how singular is the thing called pleasure and how curiously related to pain.* Candy had tried to explain the equation, but he hadn't really understood. Strange how one was now so obviously the corollary of the other, and how interchangeable they had become.

39

Leicester Square was carpeted, sparkling white, and hoar frost glistened in the trees. In front of the Odeon, snow hung about in greying heaps, and oily pools of meltwater languished in the gutters. 'God, it's cold', said Candy, pulling her fur hat down over her ears. She and Luke were dating, or at least trying it out, enjoying the novelty. They had been to see *The Company of Wolves*, a brooding, dream-like reworking of the Little Red Riding Hood story. Glancing up at Luke she recalled the granny's advice never to stray from the path, eat a windfall apple, *or trust a man whose eyebrows meet!* 'Eeek!'

'What have you done?' he asked: 'Are you all right?'

'Yes, I'm fine. I just stepped in a puddle and got a shoe full of freezing water, that's all. I was gawping at you, instead of looking where I was going.'

'Why at me?'

'I hadn't made the connection before, but you do have rather lupine eyebrows. You should let me pluck them — it might be fun.'

'For you or for me?'

'For me, silly. It would be exquisitely painful for you!'

'Thanks for the offer. I'll consider it carefully. Now, are we going to eat out or go back to my place? I haven't prepared anything, but I can always rustle up an omelette. It's my turn, remember.'

'Your place, I think', she said. 'You know Angela Lansbury is an absolute ringer for Olga Taussig.'

'Who's she?'

'My landlady … another not-so-sweet old biddy. It would be a *very* brave animal that took his chances with Olga! She'd lop his furry little balls off.'

'Why is it that werewolves are always male?' he asked. 'Adolescent girls get hairy too. Everyone has pubic hair, even those of us who'd rather not.'

'You think the wolf transformation thing is a metaphor for male puberty?'

'Absolutely! It's about loss of innocence, the implication being that all grown men are savages.'

'Then let's see if we can release more of your inner wolf', she said happily. Then reminded of Oliver, she smiled. Who would have guessed? He'd been hairy on the inside all along.

Oliver? Not a bad name for a boy …

January 1985

40

The sinking sensation began in his stomach and rapidly over-whelmed him. He was tumbling, spinning, plummeting towards Earth, but no matter how fast he fell, he never made contact. He snapped awake in a cold sweat, heart pounding, unable to move. For a while, he lay there, eyes wide open, defying sleep.

'You look terrible, Oliver', Jan had pointed out gleefully over dinner the night before. 'I think your wild women do not agree with you.'

Jan was right. If anything, he felt worse than he looked. As Darwin observed, it is not necessarily the strongest of the species that survives, nor the most intelligent, but the individual that's most responsive to change. That was essentially his problem: he was not responding well.

The doctor held out his hand: 'Ah, Mr Woolf — do please sit down.' The downward cast of the eyes told Oliver that something wasn't right. 'I'm sorry it's taken so long. I fear Christmas rather got in the way. But I finally have your results here and I'm a little troubled by them. I would like to run further tests if I may?'

'Oh, I see — troubled in what sense?'

'There are indications that you may be suffering from an acute retroviral syndrome.'

'What does that mean exactly?'

'I can't be certain at this stage. As I say, I think it would be sensible to run further tests. But you may have heard of acquired immunodeficiency syndrome? We haven't seen much of it in this country yet. They're far more familiar with it in the United States.'

'If you mean AIDS, then yes, I have heard of it. But why do you ask?'

'Is it possible that you've had a recent sexual partner who may have been exposed to the virus?'

His stomach dropped again. He had been with five people in the last three months: Nola, Irina, Jackie T, Cigarette Girl, and Liza, in that order. And then there'd been a half-hearted fumble with Bruce and the encounter with the Okie twins in the Hellfire.

'Why do you say *recent* — I thought the virus could be dormant for years?'

'It can', said the doctor. 'But typically, symptoms of the kind you are exhibiting manifest themselves within two to four weeks of contact. Have you had unprotected intercourse in the last month or so?'

'You mean penetrative sex?'

'In all probability, yes.'

Nola and Cigarette Girl, the professionals, had insisted on condoms. Nola's party trick was to hold the teat between her teeth and roll on the sheath by taking you deep in her mouth. Apart from that one night. The experience with Irina had been uncharacteristic in so many ways. He hadn't offered or been invited to use protection with either of them; and in any case, given how much cocaine they'd got through, neither one would have cared.

So, which one was it? Not Nola: she was too watchful, too methodical ever to allow herself to be infected. Then it must have been crazy, reckless, insatiable Irina. At the time he'd wanted it more than anything; to be dominated by a woman, wholly and utterly; to submit to her as if she were a man: the literal fulfilment of his darkest desire. Now he realised that it had been nothing but a crude parody. For sex to have meaning, one needed to be commanded and loved simultaneously. Without passion, everything else is worthless.

No, Irina had most likely been the warm-up routine. She'd introduced him to Jackie for the final act. Charming, seductive Jackie T, his own femme fatale. Jackie had been so desperate to try out her spiffy new vagina that, somehow, they'd kept going through the pain and the tears. The pain and the virus.

New York was probably where Bruce had fallen prey too. Except that this transaction hadn't been made spontaneously in the heat of a Chelsea bathhouse, but deliberately over a cold metal desktop in the backroom of the Hellfire.

He knew how he would end it when the time came. Not violently, like Hemingway, but quietly, in a hotel room, with whisky and Temazepam. He'd planned it carefully once when he feared he'd be sent down from Cambridge. It had two principal merits as a scenario: the anonymity of the surroundings and the certainty of being discovered in the morning.

After finding Nola's message on his answerphone, he'd jotted down a line from Rimbaud, from *A Season in Hell*, appropriately: *One night, I sat Beauty on my knee. And I found her bitter.* And still the bitterness lingered. Even the sweetness of Liza's company and the saccharine of Cigarette Girl hadn't been strong enough to neutralise the taste.

Meeting Candy had opened a window on to a sensual world that was both exciting and disturbing. A world without inhibitions or frontiers. A world to which he was too craven and too calculating ever to belong. Without Candy, he would never have discovered Nola. And Nola had led to Irina. And Irina in turn to Jackie T. And Jackie T to the virus. That left lovely Liza and their terrible, tainted love.

Tainted Love ... it had been blasting out of the sound system that first night at Maitresse. It could have been their song. Or his personal lament. Too late to run away now though. He had to tell her; tell everyone he'd had contact with. Jesus! What a mess.

He picked up the phone. Nola would know what to do. Though she had caused so much torment, in so many ways, and he was unsure how he would respond were he to see her again, he had to talk to her, if only to hear her voice at the other end of the line.

He dialled her number and listened to it ring ...

First published in 2023
by Circa Press

©2023 Circa Press Limited
and the author

Circa Press
50 Great Portland Street
London W1W 7ND
www.circa.press

ISBN
978-1-911422-40-2

Image credits
All Photographs ©Steve Diet Goedde.
Image on p.13 courtesy of the UK Fetish Archive,
Bishopsgate Institute

Captions to plates
Flyer for London fetish club, Maitresse (p. 13)
Selene, Chicago, 1995 (p. 101)
Anna, Chicago, 1996 (p. 102)
Sherri, Chicago, 1995 (p. 103)
Niki and Elizabeth, Hollywood, 1998 (p. 104)
Molly, Chicago, 1993 (p. 105)
Selene, Elisa, Yvette G, Chicago, 1994 (p. 106)
Isabella Sinclaire, Los Angeles, 2000 (p. 107)
Midori, San Francisco, 1999 (p. 108)
Isa, Chicago, 1995 (p. 109)
Selene, Chicago, 1993 (p. 110)
Sherri, Chicago, 1995 (p. 111)
Midori, Chicago, 1997 (p. 112)

Text set in
10pt Antwerp A2

Photographs by
Steve Diet Goedde

Designed by
PG Howlin' Studio

Printed & bound in
China